D1584096

Think you know it all?

Think again!

Princess Sonora knows everything, having been blessed at birth with supernatural intelligence. She is supposed to marry a very boring Prince, but she falls asleep for a hundred years instead! Then along comes Prince Christopher, who's desperate to learn why his country's sheep are all going bald . . .

SPINNING TALES

stories turned
on their heads!

By the same author

Ella Enchanted
Spinning Tales ①
The Fairy's Mistake
The Princess Test

SPINN NG TALES

Princess Sonora and the Long Sleep

GAIL CARSON LEVINE

Collins

An imprint of HarperCollinsPublishers

First published as *The Princess Tales: Princess Sonora and the Long Sleep*
in the USA by HarperCollins Children's Books 1999
First published in Great Britain by Collins 2001

1 3 5 7 9 10 8 6 4 2

Collins is an imprint of HarperCollins*Publishers* Ltd,
77-85 Fulham Palace Road, Hammersmith, London W6 8JB

The HarperCollins website address is www.fireandwater.com

ISBN 0 00 710947 4

Printed and bound in Great Britain by
Omnia Books Limited, Glasgow G64

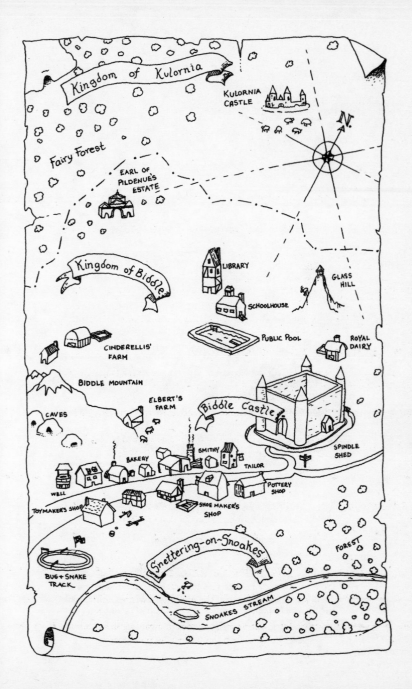

1

What a hideous baby, the fairy Arabella thought. She said, "My gift to Sonora is beauty." She touched the baby's yellow squooshed-up face with her wand.

The baby began to change. Her scrawny arms and legs became plump, and her blotchy yellow skin turned pink. Her pointy head became round.

Honey-coloured ringlets appeared on her scalp.

Ouch! It hurt to have your body change shape and to grow hair on your head in ten seconds. Sonora wailed.

King Humphrey II of Biddle thought, Why did the fairy do that? As his first-born child — as his lovey dovey oodle boodle baby — she had been fine the way she was. But he bowed low to the fairy. "Thank you, Arabella. What a wonderful gift." A person could get into a lot of trouble for failing to thank a fairy.

Queen Hermione II picked up the yowling baby and cuddled her. Then she curtsied deeply and thanked the fairy too, even though she wanted to wail along with her daughter. Sonora looks six months old, the queen thought. I wanted to watch her grow.

Gradually Sonora stopped crying, and her mother put her back into the gilded cradle. Time for the second fairy gift.

The fairy Allegra waved her wand over the baby.

"I give Sonora the gift of a loving heart."

Something was happening again, Sonora realised. But this was better. This didn't hurt. She pictured the tall being and the soft being who fed her and held her and made noises to her. They were nice! She loved them! She said, "Goo," and blew a wet bubble.

Adorable! King Humphrey II thought.

Sweet! Queen Hermione II thought.

"My turn!" The fairy Adalissia stepped up to the cradle.

Adalissia gave Sonora gracefulness. Then the fairy Annadora gave her good health, and the fairy Antonetta made her the smartest human in the world.

Not much changed when Sonora got good health, since she was healthy already. And not much changed when she got gracefulness, because month-old babies don't have much opportunity to be graceful. But something did happen when Antonetta made her a smart person. Sonora listened more closely when the nice beings thanked the fairy. She noticed her own name and knew that she'd heard it before.

Aurora, the sixth fairy, was flustered. She had planned to make Sonora the smartest person in the world, but that miserable Antonetta had stolen her gift. Now what could she give the baby? She could make the child beautiful. But no, Arabella had already used that one. Adalissia had done gracefulness. What was left? They were all looking at her. They were laughing behind their sympathetic faces, glad they had been at the head of the line.

"Er..." Aurora waved her wand vaguely. Then she had it. It was so simple. It was much better than Antonetta's. She leaned over the cradle and touched Sonora on the nose with her wand. "My gift is brilliance. Sonora is ten times as smart as any human in the world." There.

Sonora felt something happen again, a tickle and a little shake inside her head. Then — it was done. She closed her eyes to think, really think, for the first time. She listened to the noise the tall being was making. She remembered all the noises people had made with their mouths since she'd been born. Some of the noises sounded alike. Some of them always went together.

Now the soft being was making noises. They were words! The noises were words. She was thanking the fairy for her gift. She was hoping that Sonora (that's me! that's me!) would use her extraordinary intelligence well.

Sonora opened her eyes. The soft being was her mother. She was beautiful, with her big brown eyes and those lips that liked to smile at Sonora. Of course she loved her mother, since the fairy had just given her a loving heart. Sonora wondered why the fairy had done that. Didn't she think Sonora might be naturally loving?

The fairy Adrianna came forward to the cradle.

"My gift—"

The door to the royal nursery flew open. Adrianna gasped. The other fairies gasped. King Humphrey II gasped. Queen Hermione II gasped.

Sonora heard the gasps, but she could see only the things right above her, such as the pink dragon-shaped balloon that hung over the cradle. She thought, Why couldn't these fairies have given me something useful, like the ability to sit up and see what's going on?

A new fairy came in. She looked like all the others. Tall, with rubbery-looking wings, surrounded by a flickering rainbow of lights. Smiling like the others had been till a second ago.

Queen Hermione II rushed to the newcomer. "Belladonna! We're honoured." In her mind she shouted, Don't hurt my baby! Don't hurt Sonora!

The fairy looked around the room. "Pretty nursery," she cooed in an extra-sweet voice. "Cuddly stuffed unicorn. Handsome dollcastle." She looked in the cradle. "Beautiful baby."

She looks angry, Sonora thought. You didn't have to be a genius to see that.

Belladonna continued. "You failed to invite me to the naming ceremony of your only child. I suppose you have a reason?"

"We didn't invite you because we thought you…" The king stopped. He had been about to say they thought she was dead, but he couldn't say that. "We… uh… thought you'd moved away. We're so glad you could come."

"Can I get you some refreshment?" the queen asked. "We have some deli—"

"I didn't move. Nobody thinks I moved." The fairy circled the cradle. "Some stupid people think I'm dead, but let me tell you, I'm very much alive."

"We have some delicious—"

"You can't buy me off with food. Maybe you

figured the kid would get enough gifts from the seven of them." Belladonna waved her wand at the other fairies.

They drew back.

Belladonna went on. "You thought you'd economise — only buy seven gold plates, seven gold forks, seven gold..."

It's true, King Humphrey II thought unhappily. We do only have seven gold place settings, but because we thought she was dead. Not because we're stingy.

Queen Hermione II tried again. "There's plenty—"

"Maybe you thought I couldn't come up with a good gift. You thought I would run out of ideas, like Aurora here."

But I did think of a good gift, Aurora thought. How many people are ten times as smart as everybody else?

Belladonna roared, "You think I'm stupid like her? Is that what you think? Hump? Herm? Hmm?"

"Of course we don't think you're stupid," King Humphrey II said.

"I'll show you I can think of a new and special gift." She leaned over the cradle. "Kitchy coo."

Oh no, Sonora thought, wincing at the furious face. Somebody stop her! Do something!

Everyone was silent, frozen.

I have to do it, Sonora thought. I have to talk her out of whatever she's going to do. "Excuse..." Her voice was too low. She'd never said anything before. She swallowed and tried again. "Excuse—"

Belladonna didn't hear. "Annadora gave the baby good health, which she will keep until my gift takes place. So my gift to the ootsy tootsy baby" – she waved her wand – "is that she will prick herself with a spindle and die!"

When? Sonora wondered. When will I prick myself? When I'm eighty? Or in the next five minutes?

"I can't stay," Belladonna cackled. "I must fly." She vanished.

Queen Hermione II snatched Sonora up and held her tight.

Tears ran down King Humphrey II's face in rivers. What good was it being king if fairies could do this to you?

"It won't happen," the queen shouted. "I won't let it. You're not going to prick yourself with anything, sweetheart, baby dove."

Sonora wondered if her mother could prevent it. Or did it have to happen? If it had to happen, it had to happen. She'd just enjoy everything until it did. Sonora breathed deeply. Her mother smelled so good.

The fairy Adrianna coughed. "Nobody seems to remember that I haven't given Sonora my gift yet."

King Humphrey II threw himself down on his knees and clutched the fairy's skirts. Queen Hermione II put Sonora back in her cradle and threw herself down on her knees too.

"Please save our baby," the king pleaded.

"I can't reverse another fairy's gift," Adrianna said, freeing her skirts from the king's grasp. "That would cause a fairy war, and believe me, you don't want that. I thought of making Sonora artistic. What do you think?"

"Can't you do anything to save her?" the queen sobbed.

"Tutors will teach her to draw and play the harp," the king said.

Adrianna went to the cradle. "Let me think." It was mean of Belladonna to kill the kid because of her parents' mistake. "I can change Belladonna's wish a little. She has to prick herself. I can't do anything about that. I know." She waved the wand over the cradle. "Sonora will prick herself, but she will not die. My gift is that she will sleep for a hundred years instead of dying. Oh, this is brilliant!" The fairy beamed at the king and queen. "At the end of a hundred years a highly eligible prince will wake her by kissing her. How's that?"

Hmm, Sonora thought. A hundred years... her

parents would be dead by the time she woke up! She started crying and howling and bawling. And wishing the fairy Allegra hadn't given her a loving heart.

King Humphrey II picked her up. "Funny baby." He bounced her up and down. "She doesn't cry when the fairy says she's going to die. But when Adrianna saves her..." He bowed to the fairy. "Then she cries."

"We can go to the banquet hall now," the queen said.

Sonora fought to catch her breath. She had to explain. "Wait," she said finally. "Wisten!" Talking was hard without teeth. She tried again. "Listen!" There. She'd done it.

The king's jaw dropped, and he almost dropped Sonora too.

"If I sleep for a hundred years, Mother and Father—" She started crying again. "Mother and Father will die before I wake up."

"She can talk!" the queen said.

"And what if I have a dog or—"

"You can talk!" King Humphrey II lifted Sonora way above his head. "The ibble bibble baby can talk!"

And Belladonna said I couldn't think of a good gift, the fairy Aurora thought, smirking. How many gifts make month-old babies talk?

"Don't let them die while I'm asleep," Sonora begged.

She's right, the queen thought. But we can't criticise Adrianna's gift. She could get mad and harm Sonora.

"Um…" Adrianna said. If she really wanted to help Sonora, she had to fix as much as she could. "Suppose I do it this way. Suppose, when Sonora falls asleep, everybody in the castle sleeps along with her."

"Excellent," the king said. "Except sometimes we're in the courtyard."

"All right." She waved her wand. "Everybody from the moat on in will fall asleep and sleep for a hundred years." She chuckled. "Sweet dreams."

When the fairies left, King Humphrey II and Queen Hermione II had a long talk about the hundred-year sleep. They should have included Sonora, who would have had lots of good ideas. But Sonora was in the nursery, being rocked in her cradle by a Royal Nursemaid.

"Maybe it doesn't have to happen," the queen said, brushing away a tear. "We'll be very groggy when we wake up."

"We'll issue a proclamation," King Humphrey II said. "No spindles inside the castle."

"No needles," Queen Hermione II added. "Nothing sharp. Maybe if *anything* pricks her she'll fall asleep."

"No knives. No toothpicks. We'll build a shed

and keep everything in there."

"Belladonna didn't say when Sonora would prick herself," the queen said. "She could be fifty when she does it."

"No prince will marry her if he knows she's going to nap for a hundred years," the king said. "He could be out hunting, and when he comes home, nobody greets him. They're all fast asleep."

The queen agreed. "Besides, the servants would panic if they knew. The whole court would leave."

They decided to keep the hundred-year sleep a secret. They didn't think of telling Sonora to keep it a secret too, because they kept forgetting how smart she was. But they didn't need to tell her because she already knew. She'd figured it out ten seconds after Adrianna gave the gift. Now, while she lay in the darkened nursery, she was thinking it all over instead of sleeping. She'd save sleeping for her hundred-year snooze.

The fairy's gift would come true, Sonora decided. If her head could change shape and if she could become plump just because of a fairy, not to mention getting smart twice, then of course she'd prick herself and sleep for a hundred years.

Sonora also figured out that her parents would try to keep the gift from happening by hiding the spindles. But wherever they were hidden, she'd find them and take one. She wasn't going to prick herself by accident at the worst possible moment. No. She would do it on purpose when the time was exactly right.

he Royal Nursemaids couldn't get used to Sonora. It was so strange to change the nappy of a baby who was reading a book, especially a baby who blushed and said, "I'm so sorry to bother you with my elimination."

In her bath, Sonora never played with her cute balsa mermaids and whales. Instead, she'd remind the Royal

Nursemaids to wash behind her ears and between her toes. After the bath, she'd refuse to wear her adorable nightcap with the floppy donkey ears. She'd say it wasn't dignified.

The king and queen had trouble getting used to Sonora too. The king hated to watch her eat. It was unnatural to see a baby in a high chair manage a spoon and fork so perfectly. She never dribbled a drop on her yellow linen bib with the pink bunny rabbits scampering across it.

There were hundreds of things that the queen missed. Sonora never tried to fit her foot into her mouth. After her second word, "wisten," she never said another word of baby talk. She never drooled. She never gurgled. She refused to breastfeed. She admitted that it was good for her, but she said it was a barbaric, cannibalistic custom. Queen Hermione II wasn't certain what a cannibal was, but she was embarrassed to ask a little baby, even though she knew Sonora would be perfectly polite about it. Even though she knew Sonora would be delighted to be asked.

But then again, in some ways Sonora was exactly like other babies. She had to be burped like anybody else, although other babies didn't go on and on about how silly they felt waiting for the burp to come. And most babies didn't cry from shame when they sicked up on someone.

Because of her loving heart, Sonora also cried whenever anybody stopped holding her. Queen Hermione II could explain that her lap was falling asleep from holding Sonora and the heavy volume on troll psychology Sonora was reading. It didn't matter. She cried anyway. It didn't matter either if King Humphrey II said he had to meet with his Royal Councillors. Sonora cried anyway. And when the king said she was too young to help decide matters of state, her loving heart and her brilliant mind were in complete agreement – she had a temper tantrum.

She learned to crawl at about the same time as other babies, although she was more of a perfectionist about it than most. She set daily distance goals for herself, and she only crawled in perfectly straight lines and perfectly round circles. After a day of crawling practice, she once told her father that she enjoyed watching "the miracle of child development" happening to her.

Although her overall health was excellent, sometimes she got sick just like other children. Except other children didn't diagnose their own diseases or tell the Chief Royal Physician what the treatment should be. And other children got well faster than Sonora, because other children listened when their parents told them to go to sleep. Sonora wouldn't listen and wouldn't sleep.

Most nights, sick or well, she'd crawl into the royal library. She could memorise five or six books in a typical night. Fairy tales were her favourites. The more she knew about fairies, she reasoned, the better off she'd be.

On nights when she didn't feel like reading, she'd lie in her crib and think up questions. Then she'd answer them. For example, why did bread rise? She knew about yeast, but yeast wasn't the whole answer – because why did yeast do what it did? The whole answer fitted in with Sonora's Law of the Purposeful Behaviour of Everything Everywhere. Bread's purpose, she knew, was to feed people. It rose so it could feed as many people as possible. The reason jumped out at you when you thought about it correctly.

She decided that when her hand was big enough to hold a pen comfortably, she'd write a monograph on the subject.

Sonora didn't learn everything by reading and thinking. She also learned from the people around her. As soon as she could walk, she followed the Royal Dairymaids everywhere and asked them a million questions about milking. She watched the Chief Royal Blacksmith and asked him questions. She spent days in the kitchen with the Chief Royal Cook, until the Chief Royal Cook wanted to pound Sonora on her Royal Head with the Royal Frying Pan.

Once she found out everything the Royal Dairymaids knew about milking or the Chief Royal Blacksmith knew about smithing or the Chief Royal Cook knew about cooking, Sonora would get to work. She'd read every book there was on the subject. Then she'd think, and soon she'd come up with a better or faster way to milk or smith or cook or do anything else.

She'd be very excited. If it was the middle of the night, she wouldn't be able to wait until morning to talk about her discovery, so she'd wake her parents up. This was always a disappointment. The king and queen were too sleepy to listen, and sometimes they were grumpy about being wakened. The king even raised his voice once, when she woke him to say she'd found a way to grow skinless potatoes, which would save hours of peeling.

Sonora would imagine the joy her improvements would bring the Chief Royal Farmer or the Chief Royal Cook or the Royal Dairymaids. But she'd be wrong – they were hardly ever pleased. They liked doing things the way they were used to, and they didn't like being told how to do their business by a Royal Pipsqueak no bigger than a mosquito bite.

Sonora couldn't understand it. She knew that the purpose of dairymaids was more than to milk cows. They were people, and people had lots of purposes. If her brain hadn't told her that, her loving heart would have. But part of their purpose was to get milk from cows, so she couldn't understand why they didn't want to do it in the best way possible.

In fact, nobody was nearly as interested in what Sonora knew as she wanted them to be. Even her mother wasn't. Often, while the queen wrote out menu plans, Sonora would talk about her latest research.

And for the thousandth time the queen would wish that Aurora had thought of a different gift. A simple one would have been fine, Queen Hermione II would think. An excellent sense of smell would have been good, or a pretty singing voice, which didn't run in the family. She and Humphrey II both sounded like frogs.

Then the queen would try not to yawn. What was the child telling her now? How to build the fastest sailboat in the world? But Biddle was landlocked, and even its lakes were small. A *slow* sailboat could cross the biggest one pretty quickly. Queen Hermione II's eyes would close then, and her handwriting on the menu would wobble.

And Sonora would feel terrible, even though she'd know her mother didn't mean to hurt her feelings.

It would be the same with the king. He'd be deciding which squires were ready to be knighted, for example. Meanwhile, she'd start telling him about a book she'd read, a book that had been in his library forever without his ever wanting to read a word of it.

He'd say, "Sonora, sweet, we're not as smart as you are. We can't think about knights and dwindling – um, dwindling what? What's dwindling, cutie pie?"

"Dwindling unicorn habitats."

"That's right, darling. Tell us about it later when we're not so busy."

Sonora would leave then, knowing that her father hoped she'd never mention a unicorn to him again – with or without a dwindling habitat.

A new proverb sprang up in Biddle. Whenever a Biddler asked a question that nobody could answer, someone would say, "Princess Sonora knows." Then somebody else would say, "But don't ask her."

And everybody would laugh.

When Sonora was six, she read every book she could find on the art of picking locks. Then, on a dark night, she stole out of the castle and went to the shed that held the spindles and the other sharp things. The moment had come for her to get her very own spindle so she'd be able to prick herself when the time was right.

She set to work, ignoring the sign on the door that said, "Keep out! Do not enter! Private property! Danger! Get out of here!" It took her exactly twelve minutes to pick all ten locks and another fifteen minutes to very carefully remove the spindle from the first spinning wheel she came to. When that was done, she picked the spindle up with the tongs from the nursery fireplace and carried it very carefully back to the nursery, where she dropped it in the bottom of her toy chest. She left it there, under the toys her parents had got for the child they expected to have – the one who wasn't ten times as smart as anybody else.

Every year King Humphrey II and Queen Hermione II made a birthday party for Sonora, which never turned out well. The party for Sonora's tenth birthday began like all the rest. The lads and lasses had come only because they had to. They stood around in the tournament field, feeling silly in their party caps.

Sonora tried to be a good hostess and make them feel comfortable, but every subject she brought up fell flat. Nobody wanted to discuss whether fairies and elves should obey Biddle's laws, or who was happier, all things being equal, the knight or his horse.

Nobody wanted to play any games either. They had played hide-and-seek last year, and Sonora had told them how to play it better. It had taken months to forget her advice and get their good old game back. The year before that she had ruined blind man's buff.

They all sighed, including Sonora. It would be hours before she could return to her latest project, finding out why things had colours.

Then she had an inspiration. She called for ink, quill pens, and parchment for everyone. When the supplies came, she began to interview each guest in turn. Sonora listened and took notes while everybody who wasn't being interviewed grumbled about how stupid and boring this was.

When the last guest had been interviewed, Sonora cleared her throat nervously. This was the first time she had spoken before an assembly. She said, "Silence." Gradually everybody got quiet. "From my notes, I see that none of you enjoys doing chores."

The lads and lasses groaned. Now the know-it-all was going to tell them how to be better children.

"Here are seven good ways to avoid doing them."

The lads and lasses began to write as fast as they could. During the rest of that wonderful party, which flew by much too quickly for everybody, Sonora told them how to stay out late to play, how to get even with their enemies and not get caught, how not to eat food they didn't like, and how not to go to bed at bedtime (Sonora's speciality).

When the party was over, Sonora told the guests to bring their homework next year and she'd do it for them. As they left, everyone told the king and queen that it had been the best party ever. King Humphrey

II and Queen Hermione II were delighted. They told Sonora she'd be a popular queen someday.

But Sonora knew better. When the lads and lasses grew up to be Royal Bakers or Royal Chimney Sweeps, they'd dislike her advice as much as their parents did. And they'd laugh and say the proverb to each other. "Princess Sonora knows, but don't ask her."

The evening after the party, Sonora moved out of the nursery to her own grown-up bedchamber, which had only one thing wrong with it — a bed. Sonora argued that she didn't need a bed and didn't want a bed and disliked beds very much. It didn't matter, though. She was stuck with it.

Late that night, when everybody else was asleep, she used her new fireplace tongs to carry the spindle very carefully from the toy chest in the nursery to the floor of her new wardrobe. She shoved it all the way to the back and covered it with a pile of nightdresses she refused to wear.

Then she tried to forget about the spindle and a hundred years of sleep.

The right time for Sonora to prick herself didn't come. And the more time passed, the less she wanted to do it. She was only a little frightened by the hundred years. What she was most afraid of was sleep.

She hadn't slept at all since the fairy Aurora made her so smart. She'd seen her mother sleep, usually when Sonora was trying to explain something. She'd seen her father fall asleep while listening to the Royal Minstrels after dinner. Sometimes Sonora yawned when they sang, but then she'd sit up extra straight and open her eyes extra wide. She'd stay awake because sleeping people were scary. They were right in the room with you, sort of. Their bodies were, but their minds weren't, which was creepy. Sonora loved her mind, and she wanted to know where it was at all times.

∞

When Sonora was fourteen, King Humphrey II and Queen Hermione II decided on a husband for her, if she didn't prick herself before the wedding. They chose Prince Melvin XX, heir apparent to the throne of the neighbouring kingdom of Kulornia. He was the ideal choice. Kulornia was even bigger and richer than Biddle. Sonora would be queen over a vast empire.

King Humphrey II sent a dispatch to King Stanley CXLIV, the prince's father. He also sent a portrait of Sonora. King Stanley CXLIV sent back his answer.

King Humphrey II opened the dispatch and read it. "King Stanley CXLIV has agreed to the wedding," he told Sonora and Queen Hermione II. "The prince is coming for a visit." A piece of foolscap fell to the marble floor of the throne room. King Humphrey II picked it up. "Oh, look. Here's a letter from the prince." He started reading.

My dear Princess,

My father, King Stanley CXLIV, says I'm going to marry you. I believe him. He always tells the truth, so I believe him. If he were a liar, I wouldn't.

King Humphrey II nodded. "He sounds sensible."

He sounds like a fool, Sonora thought.

The king went on reading.

I believe in honesty. The fairies made me Honest when I was born. Besides, I do what my father tells me. If he says to marry someone, I marry her. I'm Traditional. The fairies made me that too when I was born. Below is a list of all the other things they made me.

1. Brave.

2. Handsome.

3. Strong.

4. A Man of Action. (I used to be a Baby of Action.)

5. *A Good Dancer.*

6. *Tall.*

Plus Honest and Traditional, as shown above. I trust you will find me as described.

> *Honestly,*
>
> *Prince Melvin XX*

"Sweetheart!" Queen Hermione II said. "He's just right for you. He's handsome and you're beautiful. He's a good dancer and you're graceful." They would have so much to share. The queen felt weepy. Her baby was leaving her.

Sonora also felt weepy. They had nothing in common. Nothing important. The fairies hadn't made him smart. They hadn't given him a loving heart. Was it time to get out the spindle and prick herself?

5

In her room, Sonora reached into her wardrobe.
She touched the nightdresses that covered
the spindle. Her heart raced. The moment had come.

But she didn't want to go to sleep.

Maybe the moment hadn't come. Maybe Prince
Melvin XX wasn't so bad. His letter was so bad. But
maybe he wasn't. Maybe he was just not a talented

writer. He probably wasn't brilliant, but that might not matter. At least people wouldn't make up horrible proverbs about not asking him the things he knew. Besides, maybe he was really wonderful.

He couldn't be.

Maybe he was. If she went to sleep now, she'd never find out. He'd get old and die before she woke up. And she'd have missed the great romance of her life.

It wouldn't hurt to find out. He was coming soon. She could always prick herself after she met him.

Prince Melvin XX came, following forty pages blowing trumpets. Sonora met him in the courtyard as he stepped down from his carriage. Probably he was handsome, but he was so tall she could hardly see his face, because it was too far away. He had dark hair and broad shoulders. She couldn't tell what colour his eyes were. She'd have to wait to see them when he sat down.

She curtsied.

He bowed. He thought, I guess she's pretty. She's puny though. The fairies didn't make her Tall.

They had no chance to talk because they had to hurry to a banquet in the prince's honour. Sonora sat at one end of the banquet table with her mother. Prince Melvin XX sat with her father at the other end.

The prince ate, chewing very slowly. Sonora watched his mouth. He ate more slowly than anyone she had ever seen before. While he ate, he talked to the king. The prince spoke so slowly that King Humphrey II forgot the beginning of each sentence by the time Prince Melvin XX got to the end. Prince Melvin XX told the king about every second of his journey to Biddle. He explained how he had decided on each item he had brought from Kulornia. He said what he had been doing when his father had agreed to the marriage.

King Humphrey II wished there weren't so many courses. Another half hour of this and he'd faint.

The meal finally ended. King Humphrey II stood up quickly. "Sonora, sweet, show your guest the garden." Get him out of here!

Sonora curtsied and led the prince away. Queen Hermione II headed for her daughter's bedchamber to see what Sonora needed for her trousseau. The king decided to take a nap.

Prince Melvin XX held the door to the garden open for Sonora. "My father says you're smart," he said slowly. "And I believe him. He always tells the truth. If he were a liar, I wouldn't believe him."

"That's reasonable." Sonora tried to smile, but she couldn't. I can't smile because I'm sad, she thought. If I were happy, I would be able to. Aaa! I'm thinking the way he talks. "Our roses are over here."

"I see them. The red ones are very red." He went on. "I'm glad you're smart. When I'm king, you can write my proclamations. I'll tell you what to say."

"If you tell me what to say, why—"

"Thinking gets in the way. People can be too smart. I'm a Man of Action. The fairies made me that way. I always know what to do. Father had to write a proclamation the other day…"

Sonora bent over to sniff a peony. Here was another person who would never want to listen to her.

The king couldn't fall asleep. His head hurt too much. Compared to the prince, Sonora was a pleasure to listen to. He rolled over on to his stomach.

In Sonora's room, Queen Hermione II began to take gowns out of the wardrobe and spread them across Sonora's bed. The child needed new ones for her trousseau. Five or ten new gowns. The prettiest gown Sonora had was blue, embroidered with seed pearls. Where was it? She turned back to the wardrobe.

∽

Sonora and Prince Melvin XX stood next to the weeping cherry tree. He was talking as usual. She had stopped listening an hour ago. He was saying very slowly that he didn't see much use for flowers. Vegetables were different. He saw a use for them. He began to list all the vegetables he could think of.

Sonora wondered how bad sleep could be. A hundred years of sleep would be shorter than five minutes with the prince. As soon as she got away from him, she'd go to her room and prick herself.

No! If she did, he'd fall asleep too, and in a hundred years she'd still have to marry him. But then she wouldn't have a hundred years of sleep to look forward to. So she couldn't prick herself now. She'd have to wait and do it when he went back to Kulornia to get ready for the wedding.

"I especially like boiled corn in the…"

But meanwhile she didn't have to spend hours

with him. She could think of an excuse to get away. She wasn't so smart for nothing.

"Do you like corn too?"

He'd stopped talking. He was looking at her, waiting. He must have asked her something.

"I'm sorry. What did you say?"

"I said do you like corn too?" Was she hard of hearing? That wouldn't be good. His own hearing was perfect.

"Not particularly." Maybe he wouldn't want to marry her if she didn't like corn.

"Oh." He shrugged. "I never met anybody who didn't like it before."

"Sir, I fear I must leave you for a while. The king likes me to use this hour for quiet meditation in my room. I will—"

"Corn might be my favourite—"

She fled.

∞

The queen lifted the last gown off its hook. Where was the blue one? Was that it on the floor of the wardrobe? She bent down to see. But it wasn't the gown. It was a pile of old nightdresses. How could the Royal Chambermaids have left them in such a heap? They could have been there for years. Queen Hermione II started pulling them out. She'd fold them up and shame the wenches with them.

Something underneath. What—

"Aaaaa! Aaaaa! Aaaaa! Help! Treason! Aaaaa! Aaaaa!" Have to get it out of here! "Aaaaa!" Protect Sonora! "Aaaaa!" She grabbed the spindle. "Aaaaa!" The shed! She had to get it to the shed! "Aaaaa!" She ran out of the room.

Sonora heard her mother's screams and thought, Spiders! She started running. Tarantulas! The screams sounded like they were coming from her own room. She thought, Black widows! I warned Father just last week. I have to reach Mother! I'm the only one who knows what to do if she's bitten.

The king sat up in bed. Was someone yelling?

The prince lifted his head. Someone was screaming. Was there a dragon? He looked up at the sky. He didn't see a dragon, so one couldn't be there.

"Aaaaa!" The queen raced down the north corridor, away from Sonora's room.

Sonora raced up the west corridor, toward her room. Let me reach her in time!

"Aaaaa!" The queen turned the corner.

"Coming! Don't wor—" Sonora turned the corner.

The spindle pierced Sonora's outstretched hand.

6

In the meadow across the moat, Elbert watched his father's flock of sheep. It was a boring job. The only time it was interesting was when the castle drawbridge was lowered. Then Elbert could watch who was going in and coming out, and he could also see into the castle courtyard.

The drawbridge was lowered now. A team of oxen

was crossing with a wagon-load of peaches. Juicy, ripe peaches. Elbert's mouth watered. Inside the courtyard, a butcher was cutting up a spring lamb. Elbert's stomach rumbled. He could almost taste it — roast lamb followed by peach pie.

On the drawbridge, the oxen stopped, and the driver slumped forward.

Huh? Elbert stared.

The driver almost fell off his bench. The heads of the oxen drooped. In the courtyard, the butcher stopped cutting. His head lolled to one side.

Arrows! Had to be arrows! Elbert spun around. No arrows were flying. He spun back. No arrows were sticking out of the wagon driver. None stuck out of the oxen.

He jumped up. Maybe he could help! Maybe he could get a few peaches and that lamb.

What was that? Something was growing along the outer rim of the moat. He started running. Whatever it was, it was growing fast — as high as his knee already. But he didn't have far to go. He ran faster. The hedge was as high as his waist. He'd jump over, grab the wagon driver, and drag him to safety.

He reached the moat. But the hedge was now up to his neck. He could still climb it, but he'd never get the driver out, and he'd get caught inside too. He stood before the hedge, panting. In his last glimpse of the drawbridge, Elbert saw one of the oxen switch its tail to brush away a fly. The ox was alive! It was — it was — asleep!

The hedge zoomed up, taller than Elbert. Taller than twice his height. Tall as the old maple in front of his cottage. Tall as the church steeple.

Elbert turned back to his sheep. Now herding was going to be completely boring, without the drawbridge and courtyard to watch.

The queen's last wide-awake thought was: The child will spend the next hundred years lying on a cold stone floor.

The king's last thoughts were: Our headache's gone. We feel sleepy. We could sleep for a hundred years.

The prince's last thought was: I could take a nap. Sleep is good for you. My father told me that...

Sonora's last thought was: Oh no, I'll have to marry him. Aaaaa!

The fairy Adrianna appeared in the courtyard. The hedge looked good. It was high and dense and prickly, with thorns as long as her wand.

In the castle she stood over the sleeping forms of Sonora and Queen Hermione II. I can't leave them on the floor, she thought. She waved her wand, and the queen floated to the bed in the royal bedchamber, next to the king. Then she moved

Sonora to her room and arranged her gracefully on the bed. She placed a wooden sign on Sonora's stomach. In flowing script it said, *"I am Princess Sonora. Kiss me, prince, and I shall be yours forever."*

Sonora wouldn't have liked that, not one little bit.

Prince Melvin XX was sneezing in his sleep, stretched out in a bed of clover. The fairy moved him to a wooden bench. Then she left without making anybody else more comfortable. They weren't royal, and they could make the best of wherever they happened to be.

In the next hour she appeared here and there throughout Biddle. She told everyone she saw that the royal family had gone on a journey. She said she had created the hedge to keep things safe while they were away.

Everyone believed her – everyone except Elbert the shepherd.

That night Elbert started building a very tall

ladder, the tallest one in Biddle. A week later, when the ladder was finished, he dragged it to the hedge and climbed up.

The peaches were brown and rotten. The dead lamb was covered with flies. But everything else was the same. The oxen stood on the drawbridge, their heads drooping. The butcher leaned over his chopping block, the knife still in his hand. While Elbert watched, the butcher lazily reached up with his other hand to scratch his nose. They were all still asleep!

But why? Elbert wondered. Princess Sonora knows, he thought, but don't ask her. He laughed. Don't ask her because she's sleeping.

Sonora dreamed it was her wedding day. The great hall was filled with guests. Prince Melvin XX stood next to her. The Chief Royal Councillor was reciting the wedding ceremony. The prince hadn't moved once the whole time. He's like a block of wood, Sonora thought.

The ceremony was almost over. The Chief Royal

Councillor said, "Prince Melvin XX, will you say a few words?"

The prince began to speak. Sonora saw a hinge at the corner of his mouth. She looked at his arm next to her. It was carved of wood! He was a big wooden puppet.

"Weddings are good. Everybody has fun at a wedding. There's always..."

Everyone clapped. Prince Melvin XX kept right on talking. Sonora screamed, "Aaaaaaaaaaaaaaaaaaaaaa..."

When Prince Melvin XX didn't return to Kulornia, King Stanley CXLIV sent a messenger to Biddle. The messenger came back and told the king about the journey the royal family was thought to have made. King Stanley CXLIV reasoned that the prince must have left with them. He wondered where they'd gone and hoped it was a good place for an Honest, Traditional, Brave, Handsome, Strong, and Tall Man of Action who was also a Good Dancer.

Five years passed. King Stanley CXLIV died, and Prince Melvin XX's younger brother, Prince Roger XCII, was crowned king of Kulornia. His first act as king was to annex the kingdom of Biddle, the kingdom without a king.

The saying "Princess Sonora knows, but don't ask her" spread from Biddle to Kulornia.

Queen Hermione II dreamed that Sonora was a little girl again. She was in the queen's lap, talking about the hissing turtle. Sonora said that the turtle hisses to fool people into thinking it's a whistling tea kettle. Then why does the tea kettle whistle? the queen asked. Because it doesn't know how to sing, Sonora explained. And Queen Hermione II thought, She's an extraordinary child.

∞

Ten years passed. The shepherd Elbert's son Elmo was four years old. Elbert dragged his long ladder to the hedge again. He climbed the ladder with Elmo in his arms. "See," he whispered into his son's ear. "They're all asleep. Fast asleep."

King Humphrey II dreamed that he was writing a proclamation making the beaver the Royal Rodent of Biddle. He wrote each word as clearly as he could. But as soon as he finished a word and went on to the next, the letters in the last word changed. For instance, "beaver" changed to "molar", and "rodent" changed to "jerkin". It was very annoying.

Every few years, Elbert's sons and grandsons and great-grandsons climbed the ladder to look at the sleeping court of Biddle.

Fifty years passed. Prince Melvin XX's grandnephew,

Prince Simon LXIX, heir apparent to the throne of Greater Kulornia, had a son. Prince Simon LXIX's wife, Bernardine LXI, the princess apparent, invited the fairies to her son Jasper CCX's naming ceremony. She invited all eight of them, including Belladonna, so no one would have hurt feelings.

There was trouble anyway. The fairies started arguing over who was the most powerful. Adrianna bellowed that she was the most powerful and she could prove it. So she turned the princess apparent into a shoehorn. Not to be outdone, Allegra changed the princess from a shoehorn into a baby troll. Then Antonetta turned her into a lady's wig. In the space of a half hour, poor Bernardine LXI became a piccolo, a crab apple tree, a quill pen, and a green peppercorn.

In the end they turned her back into a princess. But no one was certain if they had turned her into the same princess she was before. She was a little different from then on, maybe because one of the fairies had made an eensy teensy mistake, or maybe because the experience had been so terrifying.

Whatever the reason, when the princess apparent gave birth to a daughter two years later, no fairies were invited to the new baby's naming ceremony. Prince Simon LXIX worried about fairy revenge, but there was none. Each fairy blamed another fairy for the ban, so they didn't get mad at the prince, but they didn't give the child any gifts either.

And that was the end of the custom of having fairies at naming ceremonies.

Prince Melvin XX dreamed about armour. He was polishing all the parts of his armour. While he polished, he named each piece. "One polished helmet. One polished visor. One polished haute-piece. One polished pauldron." And so on.

Eighty-three years later, Prince Melvin XX's great-grandnephew, King Jasper CCX, had a son, Prince Christopher I, or plain Prince Christopher.

Even though the fairies didn't give him any gifts, Christopher had a loving heart. He was smart, but not ten times as smart as everybody else. And he was handsome, pretty handsome anyway. But mostly he was curious. When he started talking, his first word was "why". And most of his sentences from then on started with "Why".

Why is your nose above your lips and not somewhere else?

Why are nappies white?

Why do you have nails on your fingers and toes? Why don't you have them anywhere else?

Why are peas round?

Why do birds have so many feathers?

He'd ask anybody any time. The noble children of Kulornia liked Christopher, but they hated playing with him. If they were playing ice hockey, for example, he'd stop the game to ask why ice is harder to see through than water. If they were racing, he'd halt right before the finish line and ask why grass doesn't have leaves. Once, Christopher and his best friend, the young Duke Thomas, were watching a tournament. Just as the two champion knights galloped at each other, Christopher nudged his friend and pointed at a flock of geese flying above the stadium. "Look." Thomas did while Christopher whispered, "Why don't they flap their tail feathers too?" By the time Thomas looked down again, one knight was lying in the dirt and the other was trotting out of the arena.

Occasionally Thomas could answer one of Christopher's questions, but not often. Christopher's page could answer a few more questions, but then he'd be stumped. Christopher's tutors could answer even more, but then they'd be stumped. His parents could answer yet more, but they'd finally be stumped too.

When they were stumped, they all said the same thing. They all said, "Princess Sonora knows, but don't ask her." And when he asked who Princess Sonora was, they all told him it was just an expression. There was no such person.

It was the answer he hated most in the whole wide world.

8

As Prince Christopher grew older, he tried to answer his own questions. He read as much as he could in King Jasper CCX's library. He found some answers, but not enough, never enough.

Whenever his research got interesting, something always took him away from it. He'd have to practise his jousting. Or he'd have to try on a new suit of armour, or attend a banquet, where his father would forbid him to ask the guests even one single measly question.

A week after Christopher's seventeenth birthday, he was in the library, trying to find out if a dragon ever burns the roof of its mouth. A stack of books was piled next to him. He picked up the top one, *Where There's Dragon, There's Fire.* One of the chapters was about dragon skin. Did skin or something else cover the inside of a dragon's mouth? He opened to page 3,832.

A Royal Squire came into the library. "Majesty, the king wants you to come to the audience room."

Christopher slammed the book shut. It never failed.

Ten shepherds and one sheep faced the king in the audience room. As soon as Christopher took his place next to King Jasper CCX, the oldest shepherd began to speak.

"Highness, something terrible is happening to our sheep. See?" He pointed to the sheep. "She's going bald. They all are. In the spring, there won't be much fleece for us to sell."

Christopher saw big bald spots on the sheep's back.

Another shepherd said, "In the winter, they'll catch cold. It's only October, and they're already starting to sneeze."

The sheep sneezed.

King Jasper CCX said, "God bless you." Then he called for his Chief Royal Veterinarian.

The Chief Royal Veterinarian spread a smelly ointment all over the sheep's bald spots. Then she gave the shepherds a vat of the ointment to spread on all the sheep.

A week later the shepherds and the sheep were back in the audience room. The bald spots were bigger. The sheep sneezed twice.

The Chief Royal Veterinarian told the shepherds

to keep putting the ointment on the sheep. She also gave them medicine for the sheep to drink.

Two weeks later the shepherds and the sheep were back. Now the sheep had no wool left, and she never stopped sneezing.

The Chief Royal Veterinarian shook her head. "I don't know the cure," she said. "Princess Sonora knows, but don't ask her."

King Jasper CCX asked Prince Christopher what he thought.

As usual, the prince had a question. "Could we send for all the shepherds in Greater Kulornia? Maybe one of them knows how to cure the balding disease."

It was done. Shepherds came from all over Kulornia and also from the land that used to be Biddle. Four hundred shepherds camped outside Kulornia castle. One of them was Elroy, Elbert's great-great-grandson.

King Jasper CCX talked to half of the shepherds, and Prince Christopher talked to the other half. The first one hundred and ninety-nine shepherds Christopher talked to said their sheep weren't getting bald and they didn't know how to cure the balding disease.

The last shepherd Christopher spoke to was Elroy.

"Are your sheep going bald?" the prince asked.

"No, Your Majesty."

"Do you know how to cure the balding disease?"

"I'm sorry, but I don't, Your Highness. Princess Sonora knows, but don't ask her..."

Christopher turned away.

"... because she's asleep."

Christopher spun around. *What? What do you mean, she's asleep?*

Elroy told Christopher everything. He told about the ladder and the hedge and the sleeping oxen and the sleeping wagon driver and the sleeping butcher. Halfway through the story, Christopher started jumping up and down, he was so excited. When Elroy was finished, Christopher ran to his father. King Jasper CCX was talking to his last shepherd.

"*Sonora lives!*" Christopher yelled. "*She sleeps! She lives! She can tell us about the sheep! She can answer all my questions!*" He shouted to a squire, "*Saddle my horse!*"

But Christopher was too excited to wait. He ran after the squire and saddled his own horse. Then he rode to his father.

"Sire! I'm off to old Biddle Castle." He galloped away, calling behind him, "*To wake the sleeping princess!*"

After two days of hard riding, Christopher and his horse saw the hedge. The horse reared up and wouldn't go a step closer. Christopher jumped off and walked the rest of the way.

The hedge looked wicked. It was taller than the castle back home, and it was full of thick, hairy vines and thorns like spikes and waxy red berries that practically screamed, "*Poison!*"

Christopher wondered what the name of the vine was and what the berries were like. He smiled. Sonora would tell him.

It was going to take days to get inside. His sword wouldn't cut more than one vine before he'd have to sharpen it. Well, he might as well get started. He pulled the sword out of its sheath and walked toward the hedge, pointing the sword ahead of him.

It didn't touch so much as a leaf. A hole opened in the hedge and grew bigger and bigger until it was big enough for Christopher to step through.

Was it a trap? Was there really a princess named Sonora, or was a prince-eating ogress inside? Was Elroy the shepherd her messenger?

He had to go on. He had to find out — even if he died trying. He stepped through the hedge.

It snapped shut behind him. Oh no! It was as thick as before. He pointed his sword at it. Nothing happened. The hedge – or Sonora – wanted to keep him here.

He was at the edge of the moat. How was he supposed to get across? He could swim across if he was sure that the crocodiles were asleep, but he wasn't sure and he wasn't going to dive in to find out.

What? Lightning flashed out of the blue sky and struck a tree on the castle side of the moat. Whoa! The tree came down, making a rough bridge.

Christopher crossed slowly, stepping carefully between the branches. On the other side of the moat, he climbed a shoulder-high wall. Then he jumped down into a field of weeds so dense and tall that he didn't see Prince Melvin XX sleeping only a few feet away. The prince slept on the ground now. The bench he'd been lying on had rotted and fallen apart twenty years ago.

The weeds were brown and dying because it was November. Christopher wondered if this had once been the garden. He heard a rumbling. It stopped. There it was again. And again. Was it the breathing of the Sonora monster who lived in the castle?

He looked up. One of the castle's towers had crumbled, and an eagle perched atop another. Ivy climbed the walls. The pennants flying above the entrance archway were tattered rags.

Rumble. The earth trembled a little. *Rumble.*

Something rustled near Christopher's feet. Aaaa! A rat as big as a cat scampered across his boot. Christopher thought he should leave the garden. The bees were probably as big as pigeons.

Rumble.

The shepherd had said something about a wagon on the drawbridge and a butcher in the courtyard. He pushed through the weeds toward the entrance.

Rumble.

He reached the courtyard. There was the butcher! Possibly the Chief Royal Butcher, although you couldn't tell by the rags he was wearing. His shirt was so frayed and tattered that his belly showed through. He was slumped across his butcher block, next to a pile of bones. Fresh meat a hundred years ago, the prince thought.

And there was the carpenter, bent over a sawhorse, his saw at his feet. He was lucky he hadn't cut himself when he'd fallen asleep.

Rumble. Louder.

Or maybe the carpenter wasn't sleeping. Maybe they had all been turned to stone.

"Hey, wake up!" Christopher yelled. "Time to get up."

Nobody moved.

Rumble.

Christopher ran to the carpenter, who was closest. "Wake up!"

The man was filthy. His skin was coated with mud and dirt and dust and who-knew-what-else.

Christopher wrapped a corner of his cloak around his hand. Then he pushed the carpenter's arm without letting his skin touch the carpenter's skin. The arm moved! It wasn't stone. He felt the carpenter's skin through the cloak. It was warm and soft — skin, not stone.

Christopher shook the arm. "Wake up! Listen! I command you, wake up!"

The carpenter slept on. He breathed in. His nostrils flared and his chest heaved. He breathed out, and the rumble started again.

It was the carpenter breathing! No, it couldn't be. One person couldn't breathe that loudly. Christopher backed up so he could watch the butcher and the carpenter at once.

The butcher breathed in and the carpenter breathed in. The butcher breathed out and the carpenter breathed out — at exactly the same time.

There were more people in the courtyard. Two men,

possibly nobles, had been standing and talking when they'd fallen asleep. A cobbler had been shaping leather on a last. A laundress had been washing a mountain of clothes. Rags now.

They all breathed in and out at the same time. After a hundred years, they must have got into the habit of breathing together. That was what made the rumble.

Christopher went to each of them. He yelled in their ears. He shook them. He hollered, "Fire!" He yelled, "Food! Aren't you hungry?"

He yelled to the wagon driver and the oxen on the moat. But he was afraid to go to them. The drawbridge was rotting. If he stepped out on it, it might give way.

He tried to wake the dog, lying with his head on a bone. He tried to wake the cat. He told her about the huge rat that had run across his boot. The cat and the dog, Christopher decided, were sleeping because they were pets. The rats weren't pets, so they were awake.

Anyway, nothing worked. He couldn't wake anybody up.

What if Sonora wouldn't wake up either?

10

he castle doors were halfway off their hinges, so Christopher was able to open them only wide enough to slip through. Inside, he heard the flapping of wings. Bats. Birds too, from the droppings in the dust on the floor. He sneezed. He looked behind him, and there were his footsteps, sunk into a hundred years of dust. He took another step.

His boots didn't make a sound because of the dust.

It was dim in here, in the great hall. The sunlight was weak through the grimy stained-glass windows. Even the broken windows didn't let in much light, because they were draped with cobwebs.

He crossed the hall. Where should he look first for Sonora, and how would he know her when he saw her?

People were everywhere, just as they would be on a busy day in Kulornia castle. "Wake up! Wake up!" he shouted. Nothing happened. He had stopped expecting anything, but he kept trying.

He shouted at everybody. But he shook only the women, and only women who looked like they might be a princess. He didn't bother with somebody who was making a bed or stirring an empty pot. He tried not to touch anybody with his hands. The people were all so filthy.

Nobody on the first floor would wake up, and it was probably useless to go upstairs and search the bedchambers. They had fallen asleep in the middle of the day, so why would anyone be in bed? But he had come all this way, and he had waited all his life to get his questions answered. Besides, he couldn't leave even if he wanted to, because of the hedge. He returned to the great hall and climbed the staircase.

Most of the bedchambers were empty. But Christopher found King Humphrey II and Queen Hermione II on the bed in the royal bedchamber. It was sweet, Christopher thought. They were holding hands. The king snored so loudly that he probably made half the rumbling. What was left of the curtains fluttered whenever he breathed out.

Finally Christopher came to Sonora's bedchamber. Finally he came to Sonora.

Generations of spiders had spun webs from post to post of her four-poster bed. Sonora slept under hundreds of layers of spiderwebs. The prince didn't know she was Sonora. All he knew was she was disgusting.

But she was probably noble, since she was on such a grand bed, or what used to be a grand bed. She might even be a princess. He had to do something. He coughed. Ahem.

Nothing happened.

He pulled out his sword and cut through the webs, which was a mistake. They all fell on top of her. Ugh. He brushed them away as well as he could with his cloak.

What was that on her stomach? Hmm, a wooden sign. He picked it up with his cloak and brushed it off. Dust and cobwebs and peeling paint came off. Drat! I should have been more careful, he thought.

He carried the sign to the window, where a broken pane let in a bit of sunlight. The paint had flaked off, but the wood was lighter where the paint had been. He could read it.

I am Princess Sonora. Kiss me, prince, and I shall be yours forever.

He didn't want her *forever!* And he certainly didn't want to *kiss* her.

Maybe he could live without getting his questions answered. He could train himself not to care so much. He'd hack his way through the hedge even if it took a month. They could find some other way to cure the sheep.

But what about all the people in the castle? And Princess Sonora, as sickening as she was? If he left, would they sleep till the end of time?

Let some other prince kiss her. Somebody who didn't mind getting ook and yuck and vech all over his face.

Who would that be?

Maybe he didn't have to kiss her. He touched her lips with the hilt of his sword. "Princess? Wake up. Your prince just kissed you."

Nothing happened.

He bent over her. He'd do it. But she wasn't going to be his forever.

What was that on her cheek and in the corner of her mouth? Spit? Bird droppings? Ugh!

He straightened up and turned to leave. He couldn't do it. He couldn't kiss her.

11

"**P**eople float…"

Christopher whirled around. She was talking. She was awake!

Her eyes were closed. "People float because their essences…"

She was talking in her sleep. She had a sweet voice – a little hoarse, but sweet.

"People float because their essences are equal parts water and air. Stones sink..."

Even in her sleep she knew things! Sonora knows. And she was Sonora. And he was going to ask her everything.

He kissed her. He didn't think about it. He just did it. It wasn't so bad.

It was suddenly quiet. Oh, Christopher thought, they're all awake.

"Sleep is pleasant." Sonora's voice was thoughtful. "Hmm. The purpose of eyelids is to cover your eyes. If you didn't sleep, your eyelids would have little reason to close, except when the sun was too bright. But then you could just put your hands over your eyes. That's right. If you didn't have sleep, you wouldn't need eyelids, so you have to have sleep. I made a mistake before."

Christopher was thrilled. She was answering questions he'd never even thought of!

She raised her head. "It's hard to open my eyes. I knew this would happen. My eyelids are covered with cobwebs and worse, aren't they?" She sat up slowly. "Do you have any clean water?"

"No. I'm sorry."

She opened her eyes and smiled at him. "You're dirty too."

Her eyes were big and grey, and her teeth were white against her dirty skin. Her teeth looked clean. The inside of her mouth was probably clean too, so she wasn't dirty all over.

He looks nice, Sonora thought. There was something smiley about him. He was sort of handsome, but mostly he looked nice.

He bowed. "I'm Prince Christopher."

Through the broken window, they heard people calling to each other.

She stood and swept a graceful curtsy. "I am Sonora."

"The sheep of some of our shepherds are getting bald. Do you know why?"

"Baldness in sheep is caused by scissor ants."

She did know! "Really! What cures it?"

"String is their favourite food, not fleece. To get the scissor ants off the sheep, the shepherds have to put big balls of string near where the sheep graze. The ants will leave the sheep and go to the string. Then the shepherds can take the string and the ants away and get rid of them."

This was wonderful! "Do you like to answer questions?"

She smiled again. "I love to answer questions." Then she looked sad. "Only nobody likes to listen. They don't even like to ask."

"I love to ask, and I love to listen."

They smiled at each other.

The sign says she's mine forever, Christopher thought. I like that.

Sonora read the sign in Christopher's hand. That fairy Adrianna! The nerve of her! Sonora was about to say something nasty, but being so smart came to her rescue. She'd never exactly *belong* to anyone anyway, so it would be all right if the sign gave Christopher a good idea.

It did. He knelt on the dusty, cobwebby, bird-dropping-covered floor. "Will you marry me?"

Sonora started to say yes. Her loving heart loved this prince.

There were footsteps in the corridor.

She remembered. Prince Melvin XX!

The door opened. King Humphrey II and Queen Hermione II rushed in.

"Are you all right, dear?" the queen asked.

"You're dirty too," the king said. "Who's this?"

"He's Prince Christopher," Sonora said. "The sheep in his country are going bald from scissor ants."

Christopher stood up and bowed. "I am Christopher, crown prince of Greater Kulornia, and I've just asked the princess to marry me."

"But Melvin XX is crown prince of Kulornia," Queen Hermione II said.

Prince Melvin XX? Christopher thought. But he disappeared ages ago. Oh! He fell asleep too.

"Our daughter is betrothed to him. He—" King Humphrey II stopped in confusion. What did this fellow say about Greater Kulornia? Where did the "greater" come from?

Sonora said to Christopher, "Since one of the purposes of sheep is to make wool, you might wonder if a bald sheep is still a sheep."

Christopher nodded eagerly. "Is it?"

She nodded. "It is, because its other purpose is to become mutton stew, and it can still do that."

"That hadn't occurred to me." He couldn't stop smiling at her.

There were slow, heavy steps in the corridor.

Here he comes! Sonora thought. What can I do?

Prince Melvin XX came in, ducking to get through the doorway. "I fell asleep," he said slowly. "I'm dirty. My hose are torn. So is my doublet. So is my crown. So are—" He saw Christopher. "Who is he?"

Christopher bowed. "I am Christopher, crown prince of Greater Kulornia." Did Sonora want to marry this guy?

Prince Melvin XX drew his sword – *fast!* "I'm crown prince of Kulornia." But he still spoke slowly.

Sonora thought, Put that sword away! Don't hurt Prince Christopher!

Christopher thought, He probably won't kill me if I don't draw my sword. "And I just asked Princess Sonora to marry me."

Prince Melvin XX thought, I can't kill him if he

doesn't draw his sword. I'm not a Bully. I'm a Man of Action. I used to be a Baby of...

Nobody said anything. Prince Melvin XX lowered his sword.

Sonora felt a little better. At least it wasn't pointing straight at Prince Christopher any more. She thought, I can think of a way out of this. I'm not ten times as smart as anybody else for nothing.

Prince Melvin XX said, "I'm betrothed to Princess Sonora—"

Sonora had it! "Sir Melvin XX—"

I'm Prince Melvin XX. Not Sir."

Sonora shook her head. "We slept for a hundred years, so you're not a prince any more and I'm not a princess. You were betrothed to Princess Sonora, not to just plain Sonora. Right?"

"I don't know," said Prince or just plain Melvin XX.

She doesn't want to marry that great big tree

trunk, Christopher thought. But does she want to marry me?

The king wondered if he was still a king, if Sonora wasn't a princess.

Sonora smiled at Melvin XX. "Your nature is to be strong and courageous."

Melvin XX nodded. "And Traditional and—"

She went on. "You will be a wonderful, traditional knight. You can have adventures and be brave and strong—"

"And Tall."

"And tall. I'm sure Prince Christopher would make you a knight."

Christopher didn't wait for Melvin XX to say yes or no. Usually Christopher did his dubbing with his sword. But he was afraid to draw it, because Melvin XX still had his out. So Christopher reached way way up. With his naked, dirty hand he touched Melvin XX on his forehead.

"I, Prince Christopher, dub you Sir Melvin XX, knight of Greater Kulornia."

"Now you won't need me to write your proclamations," Sonora said.

Sir Melvin XX said, "I will be a good knight. A Brave knight. A Strong—"

Christopher knelt. "I've always been curious, but I've never wanted to know anything as much as this. Will you marry me, just plain Sonora?"

"Yes, I will." She nodded and took his hand. "In case you were wondering, sheep grow wool because of winter. The purpose of winter is to make ice, so people can have cherry or lemon ices in the summer. The purpose of wool is to keep sheep and then people warm while the ice is being made."

"Really? That makes so much sense."

She looks so happy, Queen Hermione II thought.

"Are we still a king?" King Humphrey II asked.

"Of course," Christopher said, standing up. He'd work it out somehow.

Then it's all right, King Humphrey II thought. "In that case, we approve of the marriage. An excellent match."

Epilogue

As soon as King Humphrey II said he approved of the marriage, a gust of wind blew through the bedchamber, and the fairy Adrianna appeared. She beamed at everyone and crowed, "My gift was the best!" Then she married Sonora and Christopher on the spot.

After they both said "I do," and after they kissed, Christopher turned to Sonora. "Do you know if dragons burn the roofs of their mouths?"

"Yes, I know. No part of a dragon burns. You see, the essence of a dragon is fire..."

And they all lived happily ever after.

The End

SPINN NG TALES

Cinderellis
and the
Glass Hill

GAIL CARSON LEVINE

An imprint of HarperCollinsPublishers

First published as *The Princess Tales: Cinderellis and the Glass Hill*
in the USA by HarperCollins Children's Books 1999
First published in Great Britain by Collins 2001

13 5 7 9 10 8 6 4 2

Collins is an imprint of HarperCollins*Publishers* Ltd,
77-85 Fulham Palace Road, Hammersmith, London W6 8JB

The HarperCollins website address is www.**fire**and**water**.com

Text copyright © Gail Carson Levine 1999
Map copyright © HarperCollins Children's Books 1999

The author and illustrator assert the moral right to be identified
as the author and illustrator of the work.

ISBN 0 00 710947 4

Printed and bound in Great Britain by
Omnia Books Limited, Glasgow G64

Conditions of Sale

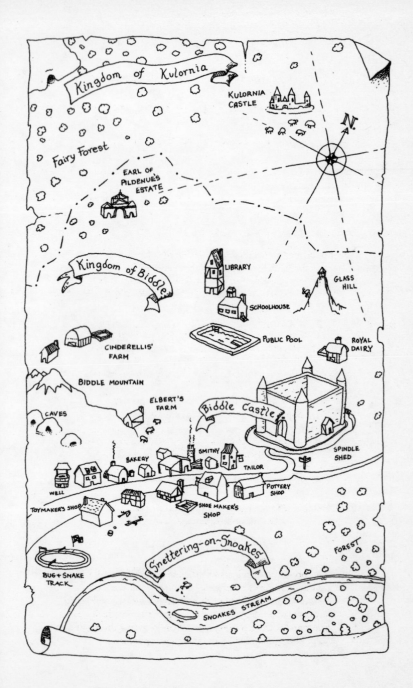

llis was always lonely.

He lived with his older brothers, Ralph
and Burt, on a farm that was across the moat from
Biddle Castle. Ralph and Burt were best friends as
well as brothers, but they wouldn't let Ellis be a best
friend too.

When he was six years old, Ellis invented flying

powder. He sprinkled the powder on his tin cup, and the cup began to rise up the chimney. He stuck his head into the fireplace to see how far up it would go. (The fire was out, of course.)

The cup didn't fly straight up. It zoomed from side to side instead, knocking soot and cinders down on Ellis' head.

Ralph and Burt came in from the farm. Ellis ducked out of the fireplace. "I made my cup fly!" he yelled. The cup fell back down the chimney and tumbled out into the parlour. "Look! It just landed!"

Ralph didn't even turn his head. He said, "Rain tomorrow."

Burt said, "Barley needs it. You're covered with cinders, Ellis."

Ralph thought that was funny.

"That's funny." He laughed. "That's what we should call him – Cinderellis."

Burt guffawed. "You have a new name, Ellis — I mean Cinderellis."

"All right," Cinderellis said. "Watch! I can make my cup fly again." He sprinkled more powder on the cup, and it rose up the chimney again.

Ralph said, "Beans need weeding."

Burt said, "Hay needs cutting."

Cinderellis thought, Maybe they'd be interested if the cup flew straight. What if I grind up my ruler and add it to the powder? That should do it.

But when the cup did fly straight, Ralph and Burt still wouldn't watch.

They weren't interested either when Cinderellis was seven and invented shrinking powder. Or when he was eight and invented growing powder and made his tin cup big enough to drink from again.

They wouldn't even try his warmslipper powder, which Cinderellis had invented just for them — to keep their feet warm on cold winter nights.

"Don't want it," Ralph said.

"Don't like it," Burt said.

Cinderellis sighed. Being an inventor was great, but it wasn't everything.

In Biddle Castle Princess Marigold was lonely too. Her mother, Queen Hermione III, had died when Marigold was two years old. And her father, King Humphrey III, was usually away from home, on a quest for some magical object or wondrous creature. And the castle children were too shy to be friendly.

When Marigold turned seven, King Humphrey III returned from his latest quest. He had been searching for a dog tiny enough to live in a walnut shell. But instead of the dog, he'd found a normal-sized kitten and a flea big enough to fill a teacup. He gave the kitten to Marigold and sent the flea to the Royal Museum of Quest Souvenirs.

Marigold loved the kitten. His fur was stripes of

honey and orange, and his nose was pink. She named him Apricot and played with him all day in the throne room, throwing a small wooden ball for him to chase. The kitten enjoyed the game and loved this gentle lass who'd rescued him from being cooped up with that disgusting, *hungry* flea.

King Humphrey III watched his daughter play. What an adorable, sweet child she was! Soon she'd be an adorable, sweet maiden, and someone would want to marry her.

The king sat up straighter on his throne. It couldn't be just anyone. The lad would have to be perfect, which didn't necessarily mean rich or handsome. Perfect meant perfect — courageous, determined, a brilliant horseman. In other words, perfect.

When the time was right, he, King Humphrey III, would go on a quest for the lad.

2

When Cinderellis was old enough to start farming, his brothers gave him the rockiest acres to work, the acres that went halfway up Biddle Mountain, the acres with the caves he loved to explore.

"It's a small section," Burt said, "but you're no farmer, Cinderellis."

"Not like us," Ralph said. He smiled his special

smile at Burt, the smile that made Cinderellis ache with longing.

"Do we have any popping corn?" Cinderellis asked, excited. This was his big chance to prove he *was* a farmer. Then Ralph and Burt would smile the special smile at him too.

He took the popping corn and mixed it with flying powder and extra-strength powder. Then he stuffed the mixture under the biggest rocks on his acres. He added twigs and lit them.

The corn popped extra high. The rocks burst out of the ground and rolled to the bottom of the mountain. The soil became light and soft and ready for planting. Cinderellis mixed his seeds with growing powder and planted them. Then he set up an invention workshop in his biggest cave.

At harvest time Cinderellis couldn't wait for his brothers to see his vegetables. His carrots were sweeter than maple syrup. His tomatoes were redder

than red paint. And his potatoes were so beautiful, you could hardly look at them. Ralph and Burt would have to admit he was a farmer.

Cinderellis sprinkled balancing powder on his vegetables and loaded them on his wheelbarrow. Then he pushed the wheelbarrow to the barn without losing even a single ruby-red radish.

Ralph and Burt were still in the fields, so Cinderellis arranged his vegetables outside the barn door. Using more balancing powder and a pinch of extra-strength powder, he stacked the tomatoes in the shape of a giant tomato and the beets in the shape of a giant beet. His masterpiece was the carrots, rising like a ballerina from a tiny tiny tip.

Finally his brothers drove up in the wagon behind Thelma the mule.

Burt took one look and said, "Tomatoes are too red."

Ralph tasted a carrot and said, "Carrots are too sweet."

Burt added, "Potatoes are too pretty."

Cinderellis said, "But carrots should taste sweet, and tomatoes are supposed to be red." He shouted, "And what's wrong with pretty potatoes?"

Ralph said, "Guess I'll load them on the wagon anyway."

Burt said, "Might as well take them to market."

When Marigold was seven and a half, King Humphrey III left Biddle Castle again, to go on a quest for water from the well of youth and happiness. Marigold missed him terribly. She told Apricot how miserable she was. Apricot purred happily. He loved it when his dear lass talked to him, and he was sure it meant she was in a good mood.

Marigold patted the cat. Apricot was wonderful, but she wished for a human friend, someone who would understand her feelings, someone who would

rather be home with her than be anywhere else in the world.

It was the end of the first day of autumn, and Cinderellis was nine years old. He woke up exactly at midnight because his bed had begun to shake. On the bureau the jars of his wake-up powder and no-smell-hose powder jiggled and rattled.

But as soon as he got up to see what was going on, the shaking stopped. So he went back to sleep.

In the morning Ralph and Burt and Cinderellis discovered that the grass in their best hay field had vanished.

A tear trickled down Ralph's cheek. "Goblins did it," he said.

Burt nodded, wiping his eyes.

Cinderellis walked across the brown field. Huh! he thought. Look at that! Hoofprints! He picked up a golden hair. "It was a horse with a golden mane,"

he announced. "Not goblins."

His brothers didn't listen. Ralph knelt and poured dirt from his left hand into his right. Burt poured dirt from his right hand into his left. Cinderellis got down on his knees too. Although he didn't see what good it would do, he poured dirt from his left hand into his right. Then he poured it from his right hand into his left.

Ralph said, "Get up, Cinderellis. Don't be such a copycat."

Cinderellis stood, feeling silly. And lonelier than ever.

3

During the winter after the hay disappeared, King Humphrey III returned. He hadn't found the well of youth and happiness, but he'd brought home a flask of coconut milk that was supposed to be just as good.

The milk didn't make anyone a day younger or a smile happier, though. All it did was make people's

toenails grow, a foot an hour. This kept the Chief Royal Manicurist busy for a week, till the effects wore off.

Marigold waited for her turn with the manicurist in the throne room with her father and all the nobles who'd had a sip of the milk. Everyone's boots and hose were off, and the smell made Apricot sneeze on his cushion next to Marigold's chair.

Marigold didn't mind the smell. She was too happy about seeing her father to mind anything — until he mentioned that he was planning a new quest, this time for a pair of seven-league boots.

Marigold would have left the room, if she had been able to walk with three-foot-long toenails. As it was, everybody saw her cry.

A year to the day after the hay vanished, Cinderellis' farmhouse shook again in the middle of the night. In the morning the hay was gone again from the same

field, and Cinderellis picked up another horse hair, a copper one.

Every night for the next year, Ralph practised a spell to scare away the goblins.

Goblins, go away *NOW!*
Go go go go *GO!*
Away away away away *AWAY!*
Now now now now *NOW!*

"The words are hard to remember," Ralph said.

Burt agreed. "Almost impossible."

Even though he knew that goblins had nothing to do with the disappearing hay, Cinderellis wanted to help. So he invented goblin-stay-away powder. It was made of dried vinegar and the claw of a dead eagle, the two things goblins fear most.

The first day of autumn came. At night Ralph headed for the barn, which was right behind the hay

field. He'd wait there for the goblins and say the spell.

"Let me come along," Cinderellis said. "I'll bring my goblin-stay-away powder."

"Don't need you," Ralph said. He smiled his special smile at Burt.

Burt smiled back. "What good would you be?" he asked.

In the middle of the night Cinderellis was still awake, because he was having imaginary conversations with his brothers, conversations in which they were amazed at how wonderful his inventions were. Conversations in which they begged him to be their friend.

At midnight the ground shook. Cinderellis smiled. Now Ralph would see that he, Cinderellis, had been right all along. Now Ralph would see the horse.

The next morning Ralph was already eating his oatmeal when Burt and Cinderellis sat down for breakfast.

"Hay all right?" Burt asked.

Ralph shook his head. "Rain today."

"Have to get the corn in," Burt said. "What happened?"

"Ground shook. Said the spell. Went to sleep. Hay was gone."

"Did you see the horse?" Cinderellis asked.

"What horse?"

"Didn't you look outside the barn?"

Ralph smiled at Burt. "What for?"

Burt guffawed.

Later that day Cinderellis found a silver horse's hair in the hay field.

The following year it was Burt's turn to spend the night in the barn. In the morning the hay was gone.

"My turn next," Cinderellis said, picking up a golden horse hair from the bare field.

Ralph and Burt roared with laughter.

"My turn next," Cinderellis insisted, turning red.

He'd save the hay. His brothers would admire him at last. And he'd never be lonely again.

A month after Burt's night in the barn, King Humphrey III returned to Biddle without finding the seven-league boots. What he had found were three shoes that walked backward, very slowly. They went straight to the Royal Museum of Quest Souvenirs.

Marigold asked her father when he would go off on his next quest. He said he was leaving in three days to find the lark whose song is sweeter than harp music.

Marigold nodded sadly and went to her bedchamber, where she patted Apricot's head and thought gloomy thoughts. Apricot closed his eyes, glad that his dear lass was happy.

Cats are so loyal, Marigold thought, swallowing her tears. They never go off on quests. They never leave you alone and lonely.

𝒞 inderellis spent day after day in his workshop
cave, getting ready for the horse's arrival. He
needed something to keep it from grazing, so he
invented horse treats. They were made of oats
and molasses and a few other ingredients to make
the treats particularly scrumptious to horses —
ground horse chestnuts, minced horse mackerel,

and chopped horse nettles.

And since horses are partial to apples, Cinderellis made the treats apple-shaped. He tried them out on Thelma and she liked them, even though she was a mule. Horses would adore them.

After he'd perfected the treats, Cinderellis turned one of his caves into a stable — an unusual stable, where the water trough refilled itself from a rain barrel outside the cave, where the rock floor had been softened by fluffy powder, and where there were paintings of subjects that horses like. Cinderellis had done the paintings himself. One was a close-up of three blades of spring grass. Another was of the ground as it would look to a galloping horse. And the last was of trees as they'd look to a cantering horse.

It was a lot of effort for just one night — because after that Ralph and Burt would probably keep the horse in the barn with Thelma. But Cinderellis

didn't mind. It would be worth everything if he could be friends with his brothers. A little extra work didn't matter compared to that.

In the middle of the summer King Humphrey III returned from his quest. But instead of the lark that sings more sweetly than a harp, he brought home a mule whose bray drowns out an orchestra.

A week later, the king left on a quest for the goose that lays the golden eggs.

Marigold noticed that the other castle children were laughing at the latest quest souvenir. Whenever she and Apricot approached a group of them, they'd be braying as hard as they could. When they saw her, they'd run away, giggling.

Marigold wished she could be a part of their group and laugh along with them. The king's souvenirs *were* funny. They would make her laugh too, if she had someone to laugh with.

∽

Late at night after the first day of autumn, Cinderellis snuck out to the barn with a bucket of horse treats. A little before midnight he heard distant hoofbeats. He opened the barn door a crack. The grass was still there.

The hoofbeats grew louder. The floorboards hummed. The hoofbeats grew even louder. The rafters hummed along with the floorboards. Cinderellis' hands shook and his teeth rattled.

Then the shaking stopped. A copper-coloured mare stepped into the field. She was the biggest, most beautiful horse Cinderellis had ever seen. Across her back lay a knight in copper armour.

This was a surprise. Cinderellis hadn't expected anyone to be on the horse.

The mare lowered her head and started to graze.

She mustn't do that! Cinderellis thought. He grabbed the bucket of horse treats and left the barn.

The horse looked up and saw an ordinary farm lad, but she liked his face. He could rescue her from the evil magician who had put a spell on her and her two sisters. The lad only had to touch her bridle and she'd be safe. The spell would be broken, and she wouldn't have to return to the magician ever again. She let the lad come right up to her. Touch the bridle, she thought. Touch the bridle.

He held out the horse treats.

She sniffed the bucket. Mmm, pleasant. She put her head in the bucket and started to munch. Yum, delectable. And the treats were shaped like apples. Great combination!

Take the bridle, lad. Please!

Cinderellis grabbed the bridle. I've got you now, he thought.

Aah! The mare was so happy. She loved this lad. She would do anything for him.

Cinderellis put the bucket down and tiptoed to

the knight lying across the mare's back. "Sir, are you all right?"

The knight didn't move.

"Sir?" Cinderellis raised his voice. "Sir? Can you hear me?"

The knight didn't answer.

Cinderellis tapped the metal. "Excuse me, sir. I hope you don't mind...'

Nothing.

He tapped louder. It sounded hollow. He lifted the couter, which covered the knight's elbow. It felt too light. If an arm were in there, it would be heavier. The knight was just an empty suit of armour! And he'd been talking to it!

5

Cinderellis led the mare to the stable cave. Inside, he lifted the armour off her back and dumped it behind a mound of hay. He took her saddle and bridle off too. Then he began to brush her.

It felt sooo good. She whinnied softly.

What should he call her? He wanted a name that meant something.

He had it. Chasam. It stood for Copper Horse Arrives Shortly After Midnight. He picked up a handful of oats and fed it to her. "Good night, Chasam."

In the morning Cinderellis led his brothers to the hay field.

"See," he said. "I saved it."

Burt said, "Goblin spell worked after all." He smiled the special smile at Ralph.

It wasn't the spell!

Ralph smiled back. He said, "Just took a while."

"It wasn't the spell," Cinderellis hollered. "I did it!"

"Time to gather the hay," Ralph said.

Cinderellis opened his mouth to tell them about Chasam and then shut it again. What if he told them and they still wouldn't admit he'd done anything? What if they said a goblin had run away because of the spell, but his horse had stayed? That was probably what they would say! And once they saw Chasam,

they'd keep her for themselves. They'd never let him
have a turn riding her or ploughing with her.

Well, he wasn't telling them. Chasam would be his
secret. He'd let them have next year's horse — *if* they
admitted that he had saved the field. He'd let them
have all the horses if they'd be his friends. After all,
friends don't hold out on each other.

To get his mind off his brothers, Cinderellis spent
the day with Chasam. He rode her, which was nothing
like riding Thelma the mule, or even like riding the
horses at the yearly fair in Snettering-on-Snoakes.
Those horses weren't as tall as Chasam was. So tall you
were higher than anybody and felt more important
too. And their gaits weren't silken like hers. She hardly
jiggled, even when she trotted. And her gallop was
completely thrilling. The trees whizzed by, and the
breeze that had ruffled Cinderellis' hair when he
started out — that breeze was miles behind. Why, he
almost caught up to yesterday's thunderstorm.

After an hour Cinderellis dismounted and started tossing horse treats to Chasam. He'd throw them, and she'd run after them and gobble them up. Sometimes she'd catch them before they landed. As time went on she became better and better, till she could catch almost anything he could throw.

It was fun, but he couldn't spend every minute playing, so he stopped and got busy. His drying powder wasn't quite right, and there had been a lot of rain lately. His lettuces were drowning.

He let Chasam graze while he did his experiments. He added ingredients that kept out water — ground umbrella, diced hood of a poncho, and pulverised roof shingle.

Chasam came over and watched.

At least someone's interested in me and my inventions, Cinderellis thought. Even if it's only a horse.

Two days before Marigold's thirteenth birthday King Humphrey III returned from his latest quest, bringing with him the turkey that lays tin eggs.

A week later the king mounted his horse in the castle courtyard. He was leaving again, this time to search for the lamp that commands a genie. Marigold begged him not to go.

King Humphrey III reached down and stroked her forehead. "But sweetheart," he said, "wouldn't you like a genie who would make all your wishes come true?"

Apricot squirmed in Marigold's arms. That horse's head was bigger than his whole body. He wanted his dear lass to step away from the horse.

Marigold shrugged. Sure she'd like a genie, so she could wish for her father to stop going on quests. But if he'd just stop on his own, she wouldn't need a genie. Besides, the king would never actually bring back a genie, so what was the point of wanting one?

6

*L*ate at night, a year after Chasam's arrival, Cinderellis and the mare waited in the hay field. Cinderellis had a pail of horse treats with him. At a few minutes before midnight Chasam started neighing and running in circles.

At midnight the ground began to tremble. Cinderellis' hands shook. The earth shimmied and

lurched. Cinderellis' teeth rattled. The trees swayed and twisted. The hay field churned and pitched. Cinderellis' stomach sloshed.

Then everything grew quiet. A silver mare stepped into the hay field. A suit of silver armour lay across her back. Cinderellis felt disloyal thinking it, but the silver horse was even more beautiful than Chasam. Bigger, stronger, and just a little prettier around her eyes.

Chasam galloped to the mare. They nuzzled. They raced together across the field. They reared up and batted each other playfully with their front hooves. Then, at last, they trotted to Cinderellis and stood by him, their sides heaving.

Cinderellis grabbed the silver mare's bridle. The silver mare was overjoyed. She loved this farm lad and would do anything for him.

"Welcome, Shasam," Cinderellis said. Shasam stood for Silver Horse Arrives Shortly After

Midnight. He led her to the stable cave. Inside, he lifted off her armour and tossed it on top of the copper armour.

In the morning Cinderellis showed Ralph and Burt that the hay field was all right.

Ralph said, "Goblins didn't come back."

Burt said, "Good year for turnips." He put his arm across Ralph's shoulder. They walked to the barn, leaving Cinderellis standing by himself.

He swallowed the lump in his throat. He wasn't going to give Shasam to his brothers either.

She was even more fun to ride than Chasam. Faster, smoother, *mightier*. She was better at catching horse treats too. But Cinderellis didn't want to hurt Chasam's feelings, so he pretended he never noticed the difference.

The following June King Humphrey III returned home. Instead of finding the lamp that commands

a genie, he had stumbled over the candle that rouses an imp. The imp was so angry about being bothered that he put a curse on the king – King Humphrey III had to go home and stay there. No quests for five whole years.

The king was heartbroken. His next quest was going to be the most important one ever. Marigold was old enough to get married, and he'd planned to find the perfect lad for her. And now he couldn't.

Marigold was sorry her father was unhappy, but she was delighted that he was going to stay home. She was also delighted that he couldn't search for her husband. It would be awful to have to marry something he brought back from a quest.

Apricot noticed the king weeping, and he worried that his dear lass might be sad too.

The day after he returned, King Humphrey III sat in the throne room and tried to listen to his Royal Councillors, but he couldn't concentrate.

Without a quest, how was he going to find the right husband for his darling daughter?

Then he had a brilliant thought. If he couldn't go searching for the right lad, he'd make lots of lads come to him! But how would he know which one was perfect? Hmm. He began to have an idea.

Exactly a year after Shasam's arrival, Chasam, Shasam, and Cinderellis waited in the hay meadow for Ghasam (Golden Horse Arrives Shortly After Midnight).

Half an hour before midnight, the wind picked up. Cinderellis felt a tremor. And another. The wind howled.

Midnight came. The ground rocked and bucked. The wind went wild, blowing from every direction. A tree was uprooted and sailed away into the east. Cinderellis' hands shook, his teeth rattled, and his stomach sloshed.

The world went black. The moon had gone out!

The stars had gone out! Cinderellis' heart bounced up and down.

Then the wind stopped. The ground steadied. The moon and stars reappeared.

A golden horse stepped into the hay field. A suit of golden armour lay across her back. Cinderellis gasped. She was gorgeous. You looked at her, and you heard trumpets playing and cymbals crashing.

Chasam and Shasam nickered. They cantered to their sister and nuzzled her. Then all three galloped joyously around the hay field, legs flying, necks stretched out, their manes and tails streaming.

Finally they stopped, and Ghasam trotted to Cinderellis. She whinnied as he took her bridle. She loved this farm lad already. She'd do anything for him.

The next morning Cinderellis told Burt and Ralph that the hay would never disappear again. He held his breath and waited. If they thanked him and smiled the special smile at him, then they could have Ghasam.

Ralph said, "Wet weather coming."

Burt said, "Maybe some hail."

Cinderellis breathed out. Nothing had changed. So he'd keep the horses, and he'd have three loyal and true animal friends. Who needed human friends anyway?

*G*hasam was better than her sisters at catching horse treats. And she was faster than they were too. Once, when Cinderellis jumped on her back, he started to sneeze. "A—" he said. She took off. He finished the sneeze. "Choo!" They had gone two miles.

When they got back to the stable cave after that

gallop, Cinderellis told Ghasam what a phenomenal horse she was. Then he told Chasam and Shasam what phenomenal horses they were, because he didn't want them to feel left out. He knew only too well what that was like.

Princess Marigold turned fifteen. There were banquets and balls and puppet shows in her honour. Everyone said she was the sweetest, kindest, least uppity princess in the world. And pretty to boot.

Nobody mentioned that she was also the most terrified princess, because she had told only Apricot about that, and he had misunderstood anyway.

She was scared because of her father and his – well, his crazy ideas. Since he couldn't go on a quest, he had devised a contest to find her future husband. He hadn't revealed the contest rules yet, but he had said that the winner would be courageous, determined, and a fine horseman. Considering the king's quest

souvenirs, though, Marigold thought she'd probably wind up marrying a mean stubborn gnome who could ride kangaroos.

The final banquet was almost over when King Humphrey III stood and beamed at his guests. "Dear friends," he began. "Tomorrow our Royal Glass-workers will begin to create a giant hill in the shape of a pyramid. It will be made entirely of glass. When it is completed, our darling daughter will wait at the top with a basket of golden apples. The brave lad who rides his horse up to her and takes three apples will have her hand in marriage."

Marigold fainted. Her father was too excited to notice. Except for Apricot, nobody noticed. They were too astonished. Apricot was worried. Had his dear lass eaten something that disagreed with her?

King Humphrey III continued. "We will also give the provinces of Skiddle, Luddle, and Buffle to the winner to rule immediately. And he will be king of all

of Biddle after I'm gone. Any lad can compete. All he needs is a horse and a suit of armour."

After she recovered from her faint, Marigold tried to persuade her father to change his mind. But he wouldn't listen. He said the winner of the contest would be perfect for her and perfect for Biddle.

Marigold disagreed. The man who won the contest would be cruel and evil. No kind person would make a horse climb a glass hill.

And she would have to marry him.

In a week the pyramid was built. Its glass was clearer than a drop of dew and slipperier than the sides of an ice cube. King Humphrey III wasn't completely satisfied, though, because it was level on top. But Marigold had flatly refused to sit on a point.

The pyramid's actual point was made by a cloth canopy that would be over the princess's head, giving her shade. King Humphrey III sighed.

It would have to do.

The king announced the contest in a proclamation. Cinderellis heard about it from Ralph at breakfast. Not because Ralph told him. No. Ralph told Burt. Naturally.

"The contest starts tomorrow." Ralph laughed. "Burt, do you think Thelma wants to climb a glass hill?"

Burt laughed for five minutes straight. "That's funny," he said.

Ralph said, "Want to see it?"

Burt said, "Wouldn't miss it."

They didn't ask me if I want to see it with them, Cinderellis thought. Well, he didn't. He wanted to climb the pyramid. He wondered how slippery the glass was.

Cinderellis didn't want to become a prince and marry a princess he'd never even met. He just wanted to see if his sticky powder would take him and one of

the mares up the glass hill. And then he wanted to show the golden apples to Ralph and Burt. They were giving up a day of farming to see the contest. That meant they cared about it. And they'd love the golden apples. They were farmers, after all. They loved fruit. When Cinderellis gave the apples to them, they'd love him too.

He took some sticky powder from his room and started walking toward Biddle Castle.

Dressed as a Royal Dairymaid, Princess Marigold wandered through the field around the pyramid. She passed gaily coloured tents and neighing, stamping horses and shouting, striding knights and squires. There are hundreds of contestants, she thought. And not one of them had even asked to meet her. All they wanted was to rule Skiddle, Luddle, and Buffle. And to make their poor horses go up a stupid glass hill.

But perhaps there was one man among them who

would be a good ruler, even if he didn't care about her. Maybe he had an extraordinary horse who didn't mind trying to climb glass, a horse so well treated that it would do anything for its rider.

If such a man was here, she had to find him and figure out how to get him to the top.

She squared her shoulders. To find him, she had to talk to all of them, all the horse torturers. That was why she had dressed as a Royal Dairymaid and left Apricot in the castle – so no one would suspect she was a princess.

Cinderellis saw the glass hill from a mile and a half away, sparkling in the sunlight. It was as high and almost as steep as the castle's highest tower. When he got close, he saw the Royal Guards surrounding the pyramid. He knew one of them – Farley, who used to sell toffee apples at the yearly fair in Snettering-on-Snoakes.

Cinderellis asked Farley to let him touch the glass hill. Farley looked around to make sure nobody was watching. Then he nodded.

Cinderellis barely felt the hill because his hand slipped off so fast. For a second it felt lovely – cool and smoother than smooth. And then his hand was back at his side. He tried again. Mmm, pleasant. Whoops!

"A lot of people are here, aren't they?" Cinderellis said.

Farley turned to look at the crowd. Quickly, Cinderellis tossed a handful of sticky powder on the hill.

"Yup," Farley said.

Three quarters of the powder rolled off the hill! If sticky powder, which stuck to *everything*, rolled off, then that hill was the slipperiest thing Cinderellis had ever seen, felt, or imagined.

8

Princess Marigold hadn't talked to a single contestant who would be a good ruler. Some wanted to raise taxes. Some wanted to have hunting parties all the time. One even said he'd declare war and take over all of Biddle! Another said he'd drown Apricot, because he didn't want cat hair all over everything! If either of them reached

the top of the hill, she'd kick him all the way to the bottom. She'd *swallow* the golden apples before she'd let either of them get his hands on them.

After talking to at least a hundred contestants, Marigold gave up. She just stared at the pyramid, trying not to bawl.

Cinderellis stared at it too. He imagined climbing it while Ralph and Burt watched.

He said goodbye to Farley and backed into a person behind him. "Oops! Excuse me." He turned around.

He'd bumped into a Royal Dairymaid. A pretty one, with a sweet face, a very sweet face.

Now here's someone with a kind face, Marigold thought. Too bad he was a farm lad. It would be a waste of time to talk to him, since he wouldn't have a suit of armour. But she wanted to know what someone who looked so kind would say.

She smiled at him, feeling shy because he looked

so nice. "Er, pardon me. What would you do if you won the contest and became prince of Skiddle and Luddle and Buffle?"

He liked her dimple. "What?" What had she said? "Sorry."

None of the others had apologised for anything. "That's all right." She repeated the question.

"I don't know." He wished he had a good answer. "I don't want to be a prince."

Ah. What a good answer. "But if you had to be?"

He wondered why she wanted to know. But why not? He was curious about lots of things too. "I guess if I were prince, I'd create inventions that would make my subjects' lives easier." That's right. That's what he *would* do. What could he invent for a Royal Dairymaid? "For example, I'd invent cow treats." He nodded, figuring it out. He'd leave out the special horse ingredients and add some ground

cow parsnip and dried cow shark instead. "The cows would love the treats, and they'd love to be milked."

"That would be a great invention," the princess said. He wanted to do something that animals would like! This lad would never torture a horse.

Nobody had ever encouraged Cinderellis before. She was the nicest maiden in Biddle. "I already invented horse treats," he said, boasting a little.

"They must be delicious," Marigold said. Gosh! she thought, he's already done something to make horses happy. "Um," she added, "if you did become a prince, would you go on quests?"

Cinderellis shook his head. "When I want something, I invent it, or invent a way to get it." He added in a rush, "Most of my inventions are powders that do things." He stopped. "You're probably not interested."

"I am! Please tell me about them." If she knew

him better, they might be friends — her first human friend.

"Well, my first invention was flying powder." He told her about the powders.

She listened and asked questions. Cinderellis had never had so much fun in his life. This Royal Dairymaid was splendid!

Marigold had never had so much fun either. She especially liked the idea of fluffy powder. You'd always have a soft place to sit, and — oh my! "Your fluffy powder could save lives. If a person — or, say, a cat — fell out of a window, you could sprinkle fluffy powder on the ground. And the cat wouldn't be hurt." She beamed at him.

He beamed back. "I'm thinking of using my sticky powder—"

"Oh no!" Marigold saw the king heading their way. "I'd better go. I have some milking to do." She curtsied and fled into the crowd.

"Where do you... When could I..."

But she was gone, and he didn't even know her name.

$\maltese$

Back in his workshop cave, Cinderellis got to work. Sticky powder alone wouldn't get him up the glass hill, so he mixed in extra-strength powder and a few other ingredients. While he invented, he thought about the Royal Dairymaid. He wished he'd had a chance to tell her he was going to climb the pyramid. Then she could have

watched and rooted for him.

But she might have thought he wanted to marry the princess. He didn't. He wanted— He stopped mixing. He wanted to marry the Royal Dairymaid! He hadn't felt lonely for a second while they'd talked.

But he didn't know her name, so how could he marry her? Well, she was a Royal Dairymaid, so he should be able to find her again. There couldn't be that many of them.

Suppose he didn't show the golden apples to Ralph and Burt. They might like the apples, but they probably wouldn't be interested in his special sticky powder, since they never cared about his inventions, not one bit. So suppose he hid the apples instead, till the princess married somebody else. Then suppose he sold them and used the money to set up an invention workshop in Snettering-on-Snoakes. He'd do what he'd said a prince should do – invent things to make people's

lives easier. He'd sell his inventions, and he'd marry the Royal Dairymaid.

He started mixing again. Yes, he'd marry her. That is, if she'd have him.

The powder was ready to try out. He spread it on Ghasam's front hoof.

She couldn't lift her foot. She strained. Finally she forced it up – grass and dirt attached.

Too strong. He cleaned off her hoof. Then he added a pinch of this and a teaspoon of that and spread the mixture on Shasam's hooves.

Now the powder didn't work at all. Shasam could even gallop. He frowned. Maybe his on-off powder was in the "off" phase when her feet were on the ground and in the "on" phase when her feet were in the air. That would mean that the sticky powder was only active when there was nothing to stick to.

He could fix that. He tapped each hoof with a stick. That should reset the phases.

There. Each step was difficult, and Shasam had to strain a little to lift her hooves, but she could lift them and the grass and dirt didn't come up too. Good.

Now he needed to add his time-release powder, which would turn the stickiness on when they started climbing the glass hill and turn it off when they got back to the bottom.

Marigold woke up in the middle of the night. She had dreamed of a secret weapon that would keep a horse and rider from getting to the top of the glass hill. With her secret weapon she wouldn't have to marry someone who was mean and nasty and cruel. She patted Apricot, who was curled up next to her, and fell back to sleep, smiling.

Early the next morning Royal Servants climbed a ladder to the top of the pyramid. They brought with them an outdoor throne, a picnic lunch for a princess and a cat, the basket of golden apples, and a water

bowl for Apricot. When they came down, Marigold carried Apricot and the secret weapon to the top. As soon as she got there, the Royal Servants took the ladder away and the contest began.

After breakfast the same morning, Ralph said, "Good day to watch a glass hill." He guffawed.

Burt guffawed.

Ralph pushed back his chair and walked out of the farmhouse. Burt pushed back his chair and followed him. Cinderellis wondered if the Royal Dairymaid would be watching the contest.

At the workshop cave, he worked on his powder some more. Finally he thought it was ready.

At first Marigold had been ready with her secret weapon whenever a horse galloped at the pyramid. But rider after rider failed to climb up even one inch, so she relaxed and became interested in looking down on

everything. The knights and squires seemed no bigger than her hand, and their cries and the neighing of their horses sounded muffled and thin. Only Biddle Mountain appeared as big as ever, looming in the distance, much higher than the glass hill.

The day grew warmer and Marigold grew hot — hot and bored. Apricot was hot too, but he knew his dear lass had brought him up there to show everyone how important he was to her. So he rubbed himself against her leg and purred.

Marigold wished she knew the name of the nice farm lad. Even if she never saw him again, though, she'd remember their conversation forever.

Cinderellis wanted to scream. He'd been putting the copper suit of armour on for hours. He'd finally got the tasset and the mail skirt on over his waist and hips. The cuisses and the poleyns and the greaves were on his legs. The sabatons were on his feet. The vambraces

were on his arms. The couters were over his elbows.

But the breastplate kept popping off!

Over and over he'd hammered it here and bent it there. And it would hold — for about ten seconds. Then *POP!*

At this rate he'd never get to the pyramid.

10

A knight on a black stallion prepared to climb the hill. The stallion looked bigger than any of the other horses. Marigold reached for her secret weapon.

But the stallion's hooves slipped off the pyramid as soon as they touched it. The knight made the horse try again — and the horse slipped again. The

knight wanted to try a third time, but everybody yelled that he should let the rest of them take a turn.

Burt and Ralph laughed so hard, their sides hurt.

Marigold put her secret weapon down and started breathing again. It was three thirty. Only a few more hours till it would be too dark to see the hill and she could come down. Only a few more hours and it would be over forever.

But then her father would come up with another horrible plan.

Cinderellis had finally wedged the breastplate under the fauld. And he'd managed to mount Chasam, even though it had taken over an hour. He'd picked Chasam because she'd looked so disappointed when he'd tried the powder out on Ghasam.

He pulled the gauntlets over his hands. Now for the helmet. Uh-oh. He couldn't make his hands in the gauntlets do anything. He'd never get the helmet

on. He took the gauntlets off again and put the helmet on.

Now he couldn't see to put on the gauntlets. He could only see through one chink in the visor, just enough to steer Chasam.

Well, he didn't need to see. He could feel. There. The gauntlets were on.

Now where were the reins? He couldn't tell through the gauntlets. Were these the reins? He hoped so.

He kicked Chasam, harder than he meant to. She didn't mind. They were off. It was five o'clock.

Two more horses to go. Marigold scratched under her tiara. She felt hot and sticky. Apricot was drinking from his water bowl. She was glad he was up here with her. She wished that kind farm lad were here too. She'd introduce him to Apricot, and he'd invent something nice for a cat.

One more horse to go.

Marigold wondered what her father would dream up next. Maybe he'd make her sit at the bottom of a glass hole, and the horse that didn't crash down and squash her would have her hand and Skiddle, Luddle, and Buffle.

The last horse, like the 213 before it, failed to climb the hill. Marigold stood up. At last. She hadn't needed her secret weapon. Wait! What was that? A cloud of dust coming from Biddle Mountain?

In the field below, King Humphrey III couldn't see the dust cloud. He decided that the contestants could all try again tomorrow. He didn't want to end the contest after just one day when it was so important.

Then he heard people shouting. There was another rider? Let him come, then. Maybe this one would be enough of a horseman to climb the pyramid. Maybe this one deserved Marigold.

Cinderellis saw the pyramid through the chink in the visor. They were almost there.

Everyone was astonished at the beauty and size of the copper-coloured mare. Everyone was also amazed that such a glorious horse would let herself be ridden by that nutty knight or whatever he was. For one thing, his armour was tarnished and filthy. His posture was terrible. His hands and the reins were flopping around in his lap. He wasn't even really riding the mare. She was carrying him, like cargo.

Marigold's heart started pounding.

Chasam cantered up to the glass hill. Cinderellis sort of kicked her to keep going. She placed her front right hoof on the hill. She leaned her weight on it. It held!

She started to climb. The watching crowd grew silent.

Marigold didn't know what to do. If this mare climbed the hill, it would be because she wanted to. Any fool could see the mare's rider wasn't making her do anything. But the rider still could be mean and

nasty. Marigold picked up her secret weapon.

But maybe he's nice, she thought, as nice as the farm lad. She had to find out. At least she had to see his face. "Sir!" she called. "Please take off your helmet."

Who was yelling? Cinderellis could see only the glass hill in front of him. He tried to look up, but all he saw was the inside of the helmet. Was something wrong? He tried to push his visor up. Nothing happened.

"I'd like to see your face," Marigold called.

Somebody was yelling again. Cinderellis decided to take the helmet completely off. He pushed up on it. Nothing happened.

Chasam was a tenth of the way up the hill. The crowd on the ground almost stopped breathing.

He's trying to do what I want, Marigold thought. That's something. And he didn't force the horse up the hill. She laughed. If he couldn't even get his helmet off, he'd never be able to pick up the apples

– if he climbed all the way up.

She thought of tossing the apples into his lap. If nobody ever got to the top, the next contest could be worse than this one. Or her father might let this contest go on forever, and she'd spend the rest of her life up here.

She put the secret weapon down. The apples were next to the throne. She took one, aimed carefully, and threw. The apple landed on Chasam's saddle, in the little valley between the saddle and Cinderellis' mail skirt.

Huh! Cinderellis thought. Did something hit me?

Marigold picked up another apple. She would have thrown it, but she got worried. She was taking an awful chance. She hadn't seen the knight and she hadn't talked to him. Maybe they could talk, even if she couldn't see him. "Sir," she called, "what would you do if you ruled Skiddle, Luddle, and Buffle?"

"What?" Cinderellis yelled. "What? Speak louder."

A roar came from the helmet. Marigold didn't hear words, just a roar. Whatever was in the armour didn't know how to talk. It could only roar. It was a monster! And she'd given it an apple!

11

Marigold reached for the pitcher that held her secret weapon. But she hesitated. She didn't want to hurt the horse.

Chasam was a third of the way up the hill. And climbing.

The monster would be up here in a minute. She had to do something! She'd try to use only enough

to make the mare slide down slowly. She leaned over the edge of her platform and poured a thin stream of olive oil down towards Cinderellis.

Everyone watching wondered why the princess was leaning over the edge of the pyramid. They were too far away to see the pitcher of oil.

The powder wasn't made to withstand olive oil. Chasam started to slip.

Cinderellis thought, We're going down! Is Chasam hurt? What went wrong with the powder?

Chasam couldn't drop Cinderellis. She loved him too much. She spread her legs so she wouldn't topple over and slid down slowly.

Ralph's and Burt's mouths dropped open. What a mare! Any other horse would have fallen on its head, or on top of its rider.

At the bottom of the pyramid Chasam turned around and took off at a gallop.

∞

King Humphrey III issued a proclamation announcing that there would be a second and a third chance to climb the glass hill.

Cinderellis lay panting in the dirt in front of the workshop cave. Chasam, Ghasam, and Shasam were grazing nearby.

It had taken him a half hour to get his helmet off. Once it was off, he'd used his teeth to tear the gauntlets off his hands. And then he'd squirmed out of everything else.

His powder had failed. He had failed.

Shasam sniffed the golden apple, which had fallen into the parsley patch. Cinderellis picked it up, and Shasam cantered a little way off, ready for a game of horse-treat catch. But Cinderellis was too depressed for games. Besides, Shasam might break a tooth on the stupid golden apple.

One apple wouldn't buy a workshop in Snettering-

on-Snoakes. He wouldn't be able to marry the Royal Dairymaid on just one apple. He might as well not have it.

Still, he wondered how he'd got it. The only explanation he could think of was that the princess had thrown it to him. But why would she?

He stood up and carried the armour and the apple into the cave. He dumped the armour on the heap with the other armour and hid the apple behind an outcropping of rock. Then he headed to the farmhouse for dinner.

Ralph and Burt were just finishing up.

"Did anyone win the contest?" Cinderellis asked.

"Not today," Ralph said. He smiled his special smile at Burt.

Cinderellis didn't even notice.

"Maybe tomorrow," Burt said.

Tomorrow?

"Or the day after," Ralph said.

He had two more chances!

"There was a beautiful mare," Ralph added.

"Mare's rider was an idiot," Burt said.

"Real idiot," Ralph said.

They both laughed.

"Work to do," Cinderellis said. He ran out of the farmhouse. He had to find out what had gone wrong with his powder. And then he had to fix it.

He'd marry that Royal Dairymaid yet!

In the stable cave he lit a lantern and bent over Chasam's left front hoof. She whinnied and blew warm air across his forehead.

Hmmmm. The hoof looked greasy. Cinderellis touched the greasy spot. He tasted it.

Olive oil! They'd used olive oil to make the pyramid slipperier. How could they do that without telling? It wasn't fair.

What would repel olive oil? Drying powder might help, but drying powder worked best on water. Olive

pits mixed with drying powder? Olive pits were surrounded by olive oil right there in the olive, and they never became soggy, so they must repel the oil. Yes, that should do it. He ran to the farmhouse pantry for olives and olive oil.

In the morning Marigold asked the Chief Royal Cook to refill her secret weapon pitcher. But the Chief Royal Cook was fresh out of olive oil. Marigold said walnut oil would be fine.

In the field around the glass hill the contestants prepared for the day's trial. A knight painted sticky honey on his horse's hooves. A squire scraped his stallion's shoes to make them rough. Another knight screwed hooks into his mare's shoes.

Outside the workshop cave Cinderellis poured olive oil down a rock that was about as steep as a glass hill. Then he dusted his new powder on Ghasam's hoofs. She started to climb and then

slipped. Cinderellis added a little more olive-pit powder and told Ghasam to try again.

The knight who had painted honey on his horse's hooves galloped up to the glass hill. His horse tried to step on to the hill but slipped right off.

Marigold petted Apricot. It was going to be another long, hot day.

Ralph grinned at Burt. Burt grinned at Ralph. It was going to be another fun day.

It had taken all morning and almost all afternoon, but Cinderellis' new powder was ready. And Cinderellis was ready, in the silver armour. It had been easier to get into, because he'd learned a few tricks the day before. But being inside was as bad as ever. He could hardly see anything, and his hands were almost useless inside the gauntlets. Still, he was in it, and he was mounted on Shasam. Chasam had

earned a rest. He'd ride Ghasam tomorrow if anything went wrong today.

But what could go wrong?

12

The sun was setting behind Biddle Mountain.

I didn't need the oil at all today, Marigold thought. But then she saw a dust cloud in the distance. Oh no! Could the mare be coming back? Could the monster be coming back?

People started yelling. "The mare! The mare!"

But it wasn't the copper mare. This horse was a

mare, but she was silver and even bigger than the copper mare. One thing was the same, though: The same fool was riding as yesterday. Anyone could see that, even though the rider wore dirty banged-up silver armour instead of dirty banged-up copper armour.

Cinderellis and Shasam reached the pyramid. Shasam started to climb the hill. It wasn't hard. She began to trot.

Marigold was terrified. The mare was halfway up the hill. Where was the walnut oil? She put Apricot down and reached for it. The hem of her gown knocked into the basket that held the apples and sent an apple clattering down the pyramid.

Shasam saw the apple. *Horse treat!* She veered and caught it with her teeth. Then she started climbing again.

Marigold poured the walnut oil. Shasam was two thirds of the way up the glass hill, but when the oil touched her hooves, she started to slip. Oh nooo! She

fought, and her hooves beat the glass.

At first Cinderellis thought Shasam was dancing. But no, she was falling. Was she all right? Was she hurt?

Shasam slid down the same way Chasam had. At the bottom she made sure Cinderellis was still in the saddle. Then she galloped away, still holding the golden apple between her teeth.

Cinderellis was furious. How could they have switched oils on him?

And what would they use tomorrow?

And how had Shasam got a golden apple? He couldn't even guess, and he didn't have time to think about it anyway. He had to figure out how to fix his powder. What he needed was an all-purpose oil repellent. On the farm they grew the nuts and grains for every kind of oil that Biddlers used. What if he ground up the hulls and pits of all of them and added that to the powder? It was a big job, but when he was

done, he'd have an all-purpose oil-repellent extra-strength time-release on-off sticky powder that would climb any glass hill anywhere.

Inventing the new powder took all night and most of the next day, but finally it was ready. Cinderellis started putting on the golden armour. It was too big, so he dusted it with shrinking powder. And made it too small. So he dusted it with growing powder. And made it too big. He wasn't used to working in such a rush, and he hated it. He sprinkled on just a little shrinking powder. And made it exactly the way it had been when he started. He was going to bounce around in it, but it would have to do. When the contest was over, he was going to invent better armour.

Marigold waited for the dust cloud. Everybody else was waiting too.

And there it was – the dust cloud.

The mare was golden this time, and so splendid she took Marigold's breath away. Why did such a marvellous horse let a monster ride her?

Cinderellis ached all over from crashing into a different part of the armour whenever Ghasam took a step. Not only that, his helmet kept bouncing around too. Sometimes he could see outside pretty well. Sometimes he could just see a little. And sometimes all he could see was the inside of the helmet. Whenever he could see, he pointed Ghasam toward the pyramid and hoped for the best.

They reached the glass hill. Ghasam started climbing. Cinderellis' helmet shifted. All he could see now was grey metal and three rivets.

Marigold didn't waste a second. She went right for her pitcher of oil, which was walnut again. She leaned over the edge of the pyramid and started pouring.

The oil flowed down the hill. It reached the mare,

but it didn't stop her. She didn't slip a bit. She just kept climbing.

Marigold dropped the pitcher and picked Apricot up. She petted the cat and trembled. She was going to have to marry the monster.

Cinderellis felt Ghasam climb higher and higher. It's working! he thought. If only he could see.

Ghasam stepped on to the platform and stopped. She didn't like being so high up. She shifted from foot to foot.

Cinderellis wondered why Ghasam had stopped. Were they at the top? Had they made it? He tried to move the helmet so he could see. He banged on it, but it didn't budge. He tried to raise the visor, but it wouldn't budge either. How would he get the third apple if he couldn't see?

Marigold hugged Apricot even tighter. Too tight, the cat thought. He wished that she'd stop squeezing and that the horse would go away.

Marigold screamed, "Stay away from us! I won't marry you!"

Somebody was yelling again. "What?" Cinderellis yelled back.

That sounds like a word, Marigold thought. But what was it? What difference did it make? She yelled, "Go away! Leave us alone!"

"What?"

She got it! It had said, "Cat". It wanted Apricot! The monster wanted Apricot! "I'll never give him up, not even if you torture me."

Ghasam wished her dear lad would tell her what to do. She took a step back and then a step forward. She hated it up here.

"What? What is it? What's happening?" Cinderellis shouted. If only he could see. If only he could hear. If only he could find the apple.

Marigold made out another word. The monster had said "cat" again, and "apple". It was saying she better

give it the apple or it would take the cat! She jumped up and down with fear and anger. "You can't have them! Go away!"

Cinderellis shoved at the visor and banged the helmet. *Ping!* It sounded like a rivet popping out, but the visor still wouldn't budge.

Ghasam wanted to go home. She took two steps forward.

It's coming at me! Aaaaa! It's going to get us! It can have the apple. Marigold rushed to the basket and snatched up an apple. Then she darted forward and placed it on the saddle in front of Cinderellis.

Apricot hated being so near a horse. He hissed and shot out a paw.

Ghasam shied back. Cinderellis bounced in the saddle. His helmet snapped back, and he stared at the inside of it where his nose should have been. The visor came off and fell on to the platform, but the visor opening was over his forehead, way above his eyes.

Ghasam shied again. Cinderellis' legs knocked into her sides. He wanted her to leave. At last. She started down the hill. At the bottom she began to gallop.

On top of the pyramid Marigold picked up the golden visor. The monster had gone at last.

But it had three apples.

13

Every day Cinderellis walked to Biddle Castle. He asked all the Royal Dairymaids about his Royal Dairymaid. Nobody knew her. The Royal Dairymaids swore there was no such person.

What good was it to have the golden apples without his sweet, adorable Royal Dairymaid? No good at all.

∞

King Humphrey III waited a week for someone to show up with the golden apples. When no one did, he and his Royal Pages went from house to house, looking for the lad whose armour matched the golden visor.

Marigold came along. She wanted to be there when they found the monster so she could do something. She didn't know what, but something. She left Apricot home to keep him safe for as long as possible.

Two weeks after the last day of the contest, the king reached Cinderellis' farm.

Ralph was weeding the alfalfa field.

King Humphrey III didn't think the fellow looked brave or determined or at all like son-in-law material, but he asked anyway. "Did you climb the glass hill? And do you have a suit of golden armour and three of the princess's golden apples?" He gestured at Marigold.

Ralph bowed to the king. "Nope."

Burt said the same exact thing when they found him in the barley field.

"Are you two the only ones on the farm?" Marigold asked.

"Yup." Then he remembered. "I mean, nope. We have another brother, Cinderellis, but he didn't go to the contest."

"Where is he?" King Humphrey III asked. Burt pointed to Biddle Mountain.

Cinderellis was outside his workshop cave, inventing armour improvements, when Ghasam whinnied. He turned and saw the king and his attendants heading up the mountain.

Cinderellis picked up the pieces of armour and ran into the cave, shooing the horses in ahead of him. Then he rushed to his tomato patch and started weeding.

The king reached the tomatoes. Cinderellis stood

and bowed. Then he stared. The Royal Dairymaid was with him. His heart started racing. What was she doing here?

It was the nice farm lad! Marigold smiled in delight.

Cinderellis wondered why there were jewels on her gown.

"Did you climb the glass hill?" King Humphrey III asked. "And do you have a suit of golden armour and three of the princess's golden apples?" He gestured at Marigold.

She was the princess? "Yes! Yes! I have them! I'll get them!" He ran into the workshop cave.

Marigold thought, He's the monster? How could he be?

Cinderellis came out of the cave, leading Chasam, Shasam, and Ghasam. In his arms were the golden helmet and the three golden apples. He put everything down and knelt before Marigold. "Will you marry me?"

He was smiling up at her. He still looked nice. But then why had he wanted Apricot? "Why did you try to take Apricot?"

What was she talking about? "What apricot?"

"My Apricot. My cat. I had him with me on the top of the glass hill."

Cinderellis started laughing. He put on the helmet, jamming it hard over his head. The visor space was over his forehead again. "I can't see anything," he said.

Marigold laughed too. He sounded like the monster. "Take off the helmet," she said.

She was saying something, but he couldn't hear what it was. Did she say she'd marry him? He pushed up on the helmet. It wouldn't come off. "It's stuck."

"Yes, I'll marry you."

What did she say?

Epilogue

In three days Cinderellis and Marigold were
married.

Ralph and Burt came to the ceremony. As soon as
it was over, they smiled their special smile at each other
and hurried home to harvest the corn.

Chasam, Shasam, and Ghasam became Marigold's
pets, just as Apricot was. The only difference was that
the horses couldn't fit on the princess's lap. Apricot got
used to the horses and even became friends with them.
He liked Cinderellis too, once he was convinced —

after a few misunderstandings — that his dear lass was happy with the lad. And he loved Cinderellis' first invention as crown prince: cat treats.

Marigold loved all Cinderellis' inventions. She and Cinderellis celebrated their wedding anniversary every year with a demonstration of his all-purpose sticky powder on the glass hill, which they kept polished just for the purpose.

King Humphrey III resumed his questing when the imp's curse ended. He returned with so many souvenirs that an extra wing had to be added to the Museum of Quest Souvenirs.

Cinderellis never went on a single quest. His only trips were to Skiddle, Luddle, and Buffle, and Marigold always went along. While there, she made so many friends that she was never lonely again.

Cinderellis' wetting powder cured a drought in Skiddle, and his drying powder worked wonders on the floods of Buffle. What's more, he showed the

Luddites how to use growing powder on their wheat crop. Everyone was so grateful that Cinderellis became the most popular ruler in Biddle history. He was never lonely again either.

And they all lived happily ever after.

The End